Topaz - an example of verve, vivacity and extreme talent!
Love ya!
Juii

SO-BRU-205

To thine own self be true and it shall follow,
As the night the day,
Thou canst not then be false to any man

From William Shakespeare's
Hamlet

And the night shall be filled with music,
And the cares, that infest the day
Shall fold their tents, like the Arabs
And as silently steal away.

From Henry Wadsworth Longfellow's
The Day is Done

Thank-you to my family, RF III and the lovers for their unconditional generosity.

Copyright © 2004 by Julie, Lady Oakes

Published by Rich Fog Micro Publishing, Vernon, BC. Printed in Canada, 2004

The sixty-one original parchment drawings, cover drawing, and three oil paintings are by Julie, Lady Oakes.

All rights reserved. No part of this work may be reproduced or transmitted in any form or by any means, electronic or mechanical, including photocopying and recording, or by any information storage or retrieval system, except as may be expressly permitted by the 1976 copyright act or in writing from Julie, Lady Oakes. Requests for permission should be addressed in writing to Julie Oakes, #371, 3104–30th Avenue, Vernon, BC, V1T 9M9.

Photographs of drawings and paintings by Richard Fogarty

Quercia Stories, 2st Edition, soft-cover, 200 copies

ISBN 0-9735795-1-X

Quercia Stories

Julie Oakes

Vernon, BC
2004

Quercia Stories

By Julie Oakes

Book One

Gentle Bondage

Book Two

Lay My Head on the Chest of the Dane

Book Three

Editing Evil

Forward

Renaissance, Sensuality and Feminism

Beauty, obsession, passion. All these describe the work of artist Julie Oakes. An artist who sees herself constantly in a state of flux. Oakes has moved from the traditionally based format, which has informed her works for the past years, toward a new format of text and image.

Quercia Stories intentionally references the techniques and concerns of Renaissance art. Over the past three years, Oakes has drawn from the Metropolitan Museum collection in New York City as a ground for her writing. She derives from the collection, yet moves away from mimicking a style, and brings the works into a contemporary framework. The materials used are the traditional media of past generations. Specific references are made to techniques of the Renaissance period: parchment paper with sepia, indigo or black pencil, canvasses prepared with rabbit-skin glue, Bologna gesso, and natural pigments. In the paintings, meticulous renderings from Renaissance works are overlaid with strange and romantic imagery, at once obfuscating and revealing. In the drawings, excerpts from *Quercia Stories* appear lightly on the page. They are difficult to read and follow. The writing is overlaid on the Met drawings with yet another layer of drawings obscuring the cursive writing. Within the universal symbols of love and eroticism the artist develops a personal, visual vocabulary.

The influence of the Renaissance features prominently in the work of Julie Oakes. It was a time of great change in European society. Artists were no longer strictly confined to religious painting. A return to classical subject matter and exploration of myths and stories presented a challenge to the artist's imagination. Not bound by fact, imagination became more important than historical reportage and figures could move freely in space.

Oakes's choice of the artist's name Titian, or Tiziano in Italian, is compelling. As Oakes has stated, she could have chosen Michael Angelo, or any other Renaissance artist, however, Titian embodies the kind of work which people easily recognize and often associate with an artist of a particular stature: the definitive artist's name. In the stories, however, Tiziano is a musician rather than a painter. Instead, a parallel can be drawn between Titian's work and the works of Oakes. For example, in Titian's masterpiece, Bacchus and Ariadne, the fable of Ariadne is portrayed, deserted in the Naxes by Theseus, who is "startled from her melancholy" by the advent of the young, handsome Bacchus, the god of wine and revelry, and his crew. Like *Quercia Stories,* presented to Oakes's North American audience, which tells the sensuous stories of the contemporary characters, Justine, Tiziano, Angelo, The Dane, My Editor and the other 'lovers,' one can appreciate the stories and the visuals without knowing the exact references. William Gaunt, in his book *Painting and Graphic Art,* describes the painting: "The contrasting movements of Ariadne and the young Bacchus leaping from his chariot impart a tremendous buoyancy and lightness of feeling... while the general plan of form and color is so bold, the subject gives Titian freedom to introduce a multitude of beautiful details: a splendid landscape distance, animals in beautiful coats, a sly faun in whose hair the artist has minutely painted a white flower." Similarly, exotic and fantastical creatures such as monkeys, lizards, rattlesnakes, dead bunnies and gargoyles appear in surprising and odd places throughout the works of Oakes, referencing historical and geographically exotic places. There is a Bacchanalian sensibility in some of the works included in this collection of drawings, paintings and stories.

The Renaissance was a period in which the discourses of representation, sexuality and morality were beginning to meet in representations of the female nude. One intriguing female Renaissance artist emerged during this time (1559), Sofonisba Anguissola, a gentlewoman who was encouraged by her father to pursue her studies in art and who was a contemporary of Titian, Michelangelo and da Vinci. Anguissola's profane portraits were highly regarded, however, Anguissola's age and sex prevented her from engaging in an aesthetic dialogue which revolves around the Napoleonic concepts of the metaphoric relationship between paint and beauty, the earthly and the sublime, the material and the celestial. Other female artists, appearing slightly later, such as Elisabetta Sirani (*Portia Wounding her Thigh*, 1664), and Artemesia Gentileschi (*Judith Decapitating Holofernes*, 1618, and one of the works that Oakes has used as a reference for her painting *Coons*), drew more freely on the classics and mythology. (Whitney Chadwick, Women, Art & Society) The Napoleonic influence on sixteenth century painting further instilled ideals of form and classical concerns. "In his Theologia Platonica, Marsilio Ficino had argued that physical beauty excites the soul to the contemplation of spiritual or divine beauty. As painting began to record a more sensuous ideal of beauty, writers like Agnolo Firenzuola, author of the of the most complete Renaissance treatise on beauty, published in 1584, described the preferred attributes of female beauty. The description of the noblewoman with fair skin, curling hair, dark eyes and perfectly curved brows, and rounded flesh recalls a number of paintings of the period, including many by Titian."(Whitney Chadwick, Women, Art & Society)

In these works, Oakes searches for the 21st century perfect form: male and female, the images projected are idealized. With the addition of images of woman's lingerie, the traditional, conservative view of female sexuality, where the female is on display and adorned for the pleasure of the male, is illustrated most evidently in the series of drawings. Here, a leg is measured, exposed and presented before a fully dressed male; a mask hides an identity, real or imagined, and is removed. The difference is in the confidence of the women, for both Justine, the 21st century confessor of *Quercia Stories*, and Julie Oakes, who tells Justine's story are women acting as full and participating partners in the process, both in sex and art making. Unlike female artists working in the Renaissance period, Oakes is free to explore her own sensuality with confidence and a lack of embarrassment.

The bed is an image clearly charged with sexual, political and sociological symbolism. *Quercia Stories* are tales of beddings. On first reading, the overall images are layered, yet they are also often broken down into fragments, reconstituted, and scaled toward the intimate. Erotic references from historical works, Victorian illustration, East Indian Tantric paintings, or Japanese erotica offer titillation, with contemporary images such as the provocative stiletto, lacy underwear, lipstick or the feathery fronds of an artist's brush balancing the collection with a less specific representation of sensuality. The freedom of literary expression, the strong, graphic presentation and the artist's confidence in handling her materials works well with the duplicity of the imagery: romance and threat, life and death, love and its absence.

At once feminine and masculine, hard-edged and soft, *Quercia Stories*, as a whole, text and visuals, captures the enigma that is the often tenuous and volatile relationship between human beings.

Susan Brandoli
Director/Curator,
Vernon Public Art Gallery

Consuming Moths
Justine Tells Juliette All

I am obsessively drawn to the potent seduction of sexuality. Sexual encounters consume my interest, time and energy. My research drives my desire to know more, to tell more, and to critically theorize.

I emerged from the cocoon of a twenty-year marriage with sufficient physical beauty to still attract lovers. I love having sex. I mistrust "being in love" or any attachment based on habit, duty or a domesticated sexuality. I am able to use my body with a degree of objectivity to increase a seduction. I tilt my hip for effect, arch my back to showcase my ass and reveal the length of my leg in a black stocking with a lacey edge. I flirt. I am not, however, a coquette. I am a mature, hot-blooded woman, flaming and flaring, giving heat and consuming moths.

These tales of sexual encounters issue from a construct that precludes a domestic potential. The stories are not about mating rituals. My lovers are married men, younger and far younger men - men who will not be in the same place as I am in a year's time.

These stories of *jouissance* won't blind you. Hairs will not grow from your palms as you turn the pages. You may decide to hold the book in your left hand in order to free your right to enjoy the feel of your own liquid folds or engorged member. Your fingers could conduct their own research, for analysis of the reference to the phallus apparently leads to this necessity.

You may think you recognize in these stories the identity of my sexual partners. You may believe you are one of them. To the contrary, the integrity of this research is built on the premise that the lovers are not knowable. The whole truth is what cannot be told. It is what can only be told on the condition that one doesn't push it to the edge, that one only half tells it.

I am humble before my task. I count my lucky stars, the lovers. I feel privileged. My eyes are wide, wild and *sanpaku* with the effort required to conduct this research.

Book One
Gentle Bondage

Death of Harmonia,
oil on canvas, 60"x 54"

Chapter One
Angiolo
Normalemente

The first story begins in Venice, with a man's voice.

"Sono forte, sono forte," the men pound the pylons into the lagoon clay of Venice. The city is built on an inverted forest of pilings brought from the mainland since the seventh century. They support the *Piazza San Marco*, the church of *San Giovanni e Paolo* and the apartment I rent, built in the seventeenth century. My ceiling is the same wood that was there when Napoleon entered Venice and the republic of one thousand years drew to a close. The men's voices echo across the canal. It is Saturday and the residential sectors of Venice are quiet. *San Marco* and the *Rialto* will be swarming with poorly dressed tourists, unaware of the offense they are causing the Italians as they wander, barely covered, through the streets of the most elegant city in the world.

I am lost in the labyrinth trying to find *La Chiesa di San Giovanni e Paolo.* I ask directions at a restaurant that is closing for the afternoon and a voice from the cool darkness offers to walk in that direction with me. Angiolo emerges.

Angiolo is darker than Latin. He has the coloring of the Moor depicted in the Veronese in the *Accademia Gallery.* He is still learning English. His definition for "ambition" is "sacrifice."

He says, "Americans live for work and the Italians work for live."

He embraces the word *normalemente* as a reason to respond to the immediacy of life. He works very hard, he tells me, but he believes that it is good to work hard. It is *normalemente.* He spent four years studying medicine at the university in Padua but didn't finish because he had to work to support his mother. He likes his work. He is a waiter in his Uncle's restaurant. His face rests in an impenetrable expression that carries a look of the knowledge of his ancestry, the Moors, who began as slaves like the caryatids in the Friari church - four black, granite, massive bodies with white, marble, ragged clothing. His virile body relaxes in the well-cut Italian clothes. He embraces his masculinity and wants to have children. All men want to have children he says. It is *normalemente.* His hair is blue-jet-black curled tight and stiff with gel. He says I am beautiful and that he knows I am older than he is but what does this matter. He likes me. I have a beautiful face, a beautiful body; of course he must say I am beautiful. He is a young man. It is *normalemente.*

We drink *prosecco*, a Venetian champagne and Angiolo takes my phone number, before I enter the church. Two days later he calls and asks if I can join him for dinner.

At eleven in the evening, I walk out of church after hearing Vivaldi's "Four Seasons" performed by the Academy of Music. I have spent the past hour in an intimate eye contact with an enigmatic cello player.

Angiolo stands beside the statue of *San Bartholomeo*, a cream suit jacket draped across his shoulder like the statue's white marble, like a Venetian carnival cape. He saunters towards me, on his own agenda, his thoughts on a private dusky path. Physically, he is truly a beauty. His shirt is open and I can see the gold necklaces given to him by his mother, a charm of tiny hearts and keys and a letter "F" for his surname, twisted and tangled, nestling in the black curly hairs on his chest, glistening with a light glaze of night sweat. He has just finished an eight hour evening shift at the restaurant. He is twenty eight years old, possesses composure, reeks of style and oozes sex. We eat a little and then walk over the deserted midnight Rialto Bridge and enter the labyrinth.

Angiolo asks if I would like to see something special and takes my hand to lead down a small alleyway, past Dante's house and under a *sorto portego*, a low portal between the buildings where the damp smell of Venetian bricks clings to our hair as we duck through. We are on a small canal with no bridge across and no access other than the one we have come in by. The shutters are closed. There are no lights. He draws me to his warm damp chest and kisses me.

In the opera *Tosca,* the kiss of Tosca, *il baccio di Tosca*, was full, fatal, female and proclaimed at full volume as she plunged her knife into the heart of the captor of her beloved Mario. When she discovers Mario has died she cries "Mario, Mario!" The kiss from Angiolo Fabrini, this night in Venice, echoes "Angiolo, Angiolo!" The sound of his full, delicious lips rings along the canals like morning church bells.

The aristocrats stir beneath their embroidered Venetian covers behind Burano lace at windows shuttered in old gilt. Angiolo slips his hand up my skirt and draws aside the lace thong to touch my sex with his finger. I tell him I am bleeding and he moans. I unzip his cream pants and draw out his hard Moorish cock. We never draw another breath, our lips glued together, his tongue fills my mouth and his silky lashes flutter on my cheek as he comes in my hand, on the front of my sweater and on my skirt slit to the thigh.

We come out of the dark alley to a dim square and he leaves me.

I walk home alone. I see the looks on the faces of the Germans still drinking by the light of the cafe as I pass by their table. I see them look at the cum on my black Italian sweater as my heels tap home on the stones laid down by the Moors.

Chapter Two
Tiziano
Gulped Beauty

I have become Tiziano's Canadian mistress.
He divides his life between Venice and Boston. His mother and father were Italian and he speaks the language perfectly which has seduced me. Most of his childhood has been spent in Boston. I met him the first summer I spent in Venice when I frequented the Vivaldi concertos hosted by the *Acaddemia di Musica*. I heard him play from "The Four Seasons" on the night of my first date with Angiolo.

Tiziano is the cello player for the summer concerts in Venice and in the winter, the principal cellist for the Boston Philharmonic Symphony. His eyes are limpid, distracted by his private melodies. He is worldly and sophisticated. His black Italian hair has a shocking stripe of white in the front, following a defined widow's peak. His aspect is aristocratic.

I am bold. I have no time to waste. After three concertos of riveting concentrated allure, I invite him to lunch.

We talk about our lives. I tell him the story of my divorce and he is amazed by the alcoholic behavior of my ex-husband. I tell him of my winter romances. He tells me of his children. He has two girls and a boy who stay with his American wife in Boston while he plays in the churches of Venice during the tourist season. He says he is very happy with his life.

I say that I am very happy with mine.

I tell him I would like to sleep with him, in order to know him better. He understands this, and had thought of it as well, during the concertos. He had repeatedly drawn his bow back and forth, dedicating the movement to musing about the redheaded woman who always secured a reserved seat He is concerned though, about his public reputation.

I reiterate that I want to be close to him, perhaps just lie down together and not have sex, that I understand his concern.

As I walk home after our lunch, I savor the labyrinth. I savor the memory of our lunch together and mull over the words we have exchanged. I yield to the temptation to pass by his apartment, the doorway beside Dante's house. I turn the last corner to approach the seventeenth century building from the end of a long narrow *strada*. Light is illuminating his door as it falls through the narrow passage way to the right. The shutters of the windows above are open.

He is in.

I come into the cool white foyer with the terrazzo floor. The shutters are closed. It is hushed. I walk out and then back into the cool entrance. I stand outside his door but don't knock. Then I leave quietly. From my home, I telephone him. He invites me over. That is the last legitimate memory.

I believe that during the life of an artist, a poet, a dancer there will be lovers. The lovers, too, will be poets or musicians, artists or actors. They will be great lovers because they are true musicians, poets, dancers and artists. The simpatico is so great that it reveals they are lovers. They don't have to stay or remain true or continue. They just have to come and their beauty is revealed.

Tiziano's beauty is delicate and fragile. He is exhausted and sweating, sweetly damp. His penis is long under loose, cotton clothing. It is easy to find. He is there to hold.

His hands, pressing my back in, find my silk panties, His eyes close. His mouth opens. His skin is so soft that I can feel his skull's hollows. He is abandoned, fragile and sensitive. He yields like a baby.

I suck on his cock. He comes and he comes, so much cum that I marvel. He faints, he weakens, he says *"si, si, si."* He makes noises, dove noises; and pumps, palpitates, cum.

I am satisfied. I have seen how he comes.

I can't have him. I don't want to own him.

I was there when he came. I gulped down his beauty and tasted his breath.

I leave for my next lecture. I will be late, walking into the lecture hall with no one realizing what I have just done, or with whom I have just done it.

7

There is a slide presentation and the seats are full. I walk to the front where Bartlett is lying on the carpet looking up at the screen. In order to get to the free space I will have to step over his face in my long leopard print dress. He will notice my presence as my scent passes over his face. This could be risky. The risk lies in affronting Bartlett, offending his sense of decency, of which I have no idea.

I whisper to Bartlett to move, please, or I will have to step over him.

He replies, "well that could be interesting," with no indication as to whether he would have rejected the pass or accepted it.

People repress jouissance because it is not fitting for it to be spoken... it is inappropriate.

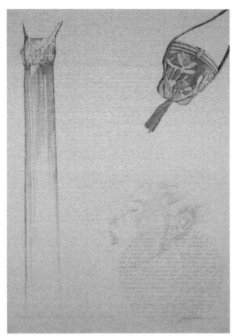

Chapter Three
Ben
The Letters

My lover in Canada writes to me during the time I am with my Italian lover. The letters are descriptions of my body and of the sexual experiences we have enjoyed together. They are letters of lust and betrayal. The betrayal consists of his having read the emails I had exchanged with the poet before I had left Canada. The discovery of my email exchange with the poet revealed just how hot and heavy it had become.

The letters from my jealous Canadian lover create a subtext throughout the summer. They become the backgrounds for every drawing that I execute. I prepare the drawing surface by hand copying the letters onto a sheet of parchment paper; then I draw objects from my present experience on top of the writing. The objects signify the Venetian sexual encounters.

Although I like receiving the letters, for they are flattering and titillating, I resent them. I want to be absolutely free to change and explore. The letters intimidate me. I am too conversant with guilt. It runs throughout my statement.

The white paper missives create holes in the delicate lacey order and sweep the web away that so easily grows from my belly. This far, distant lover still feels my bite, a raw red itch that activates his life. He is determined to scratch. The sticky gossamer threads lend him a perverse comfort. A new web, to him, is not tolerable for it would provide me with new nourishment. It would pass through my body and send out fresh designs to be decorated with dew.

I am drawing over his personality, shrouded as it is in my seduction. I draw an image that is seated in unadulterated freedom of expression. My Italian lover is an iridescent, shining prize absolutely impossible to gum up. I can taste him when he deigns to land, but I am not allowed to spin in his house. There is no need for him to cure me of my habitual weaving. He has his house and my web is not a part of it.

I am confused as to who is in the fly position as I arrive home to a letter in the green heavy mailbox on the inside of my thick wooden door. I sit in the cool, read the letter and slide to my knees on the terrazzo floor. I roll onto my back and with the cold hard relief as a naked bed, *I fondle the memory* of my Canadian lover. I rewrite his letter as a backdrop for a new drawing and wander to the window looking out to the garden, a courtyard cooled by banana leaves. I pull up my dress and slip my fingers in my panties. His humongous size came through the letters. *I moan his name in his absence.*

Call me one, him another fly. We are tapers too, and illuminate by our actions.

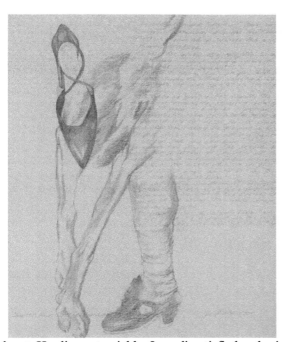

Chapter Four
Tiziano
Hungry Love

Having an unattainable lover leaves me on edge. I circle around my thoughts of him. I am dissatisfied and alive. He is married.
When a lover satiates me I move slowly. I feel dopey and drugged. I don't want to be reminded of him. He's a habitual lover.

My unattainable lover moves quickly. I want to stop him long enough to really look at him, to grab his shoulders and smooch him with big, juicy kisses but his eyes close when I kiss him. His penis is long and thin to penetrate and pierce my heart. He slips out quickly. I am dissatisfied and pricked to the quick, awakened to my need.

I have to hold off my Canadian lover, who satiates me, for fear he will consume me, eat me alive. He is able to consume me for he is strong. With him, I am in danger of being too full, eating too much, falling asleep and never again waking up.

I must stay lean to survive. When my belly's not full I can imagine eating. I am motivated to find food.

If I believe I am beautiful, I no longer try for beauty. I lose my beauty.

I suspect I am superficial so I strive for depth.

"You want I should take you?" said in the language of intimacy from the eighteenth century, in a room which reflects his antique Italian heritage.

"I like the shoes. Are they the shoes in the painting? I don't have a condom. Could you put on the shoes?"

I put on the shoes, black strappy high heels. We move slowly this time, watching, in order to save it. Our eyes are wide open as we savor the touching.

His body is perfect. He's small. His gestures are dramatic, assured and generous. He uses my body as a prop in his narrative. He holds me like a bride being carried over the threshold. He cradles me on his lap facing backwards, a high-heeled whore. He takes off my panties.

We go into my bedroom. The window opens directly onto the street. We close the shutters. He startles at the street sounds outside of the dimness. He notices the bottle of wine in the corner that I have saved for a friend. The idea delights him.

He puts on a condom. It is tight on his penis. For me it is too much between us. I respond to his being, the thrusts of his being. He comes deep inside me. I echo.

He brushes the shock of white hair back off his forehead. He looks at me for a long time.

"Just this one time, for our memories," he whispers.

Chapter Five
Tiziano
Heightened by the Rain

"Love hurts. Love mars. Love wounds and scars. Any heart not tough or strong enough - to take a lot of pain, take a lot of pain - love is like a flood, heightened by the rain."
I can hear the words of "Love Hurts," the classic blues song. Today it belongs to me.

Each time it becomes more difficult. The next day I feel so tired. I can't sleep at night. His strokes haunt me. We are swimming in deep waters. I can see the panic in his eyes as his strokes draw us towards a deeper surrender. I can sense his concern as we come back to shore.

I want to go deeper. I want his naked penis in me. I want to dive headfirst together.

We are so alike, darters, moving fast through the day, barely alighting. It is a challenge to sit through the concerto, to suspend our mutual adoration. He is the inspired darling of the doting audiences. They are there to listen to the purity of his passionate rendering of the work of a composer, now dead, who has not tasted the lips of a woman since the eighteenth century. Tiziano is tired, haunted by our midnight skinny dip. He looks towards me with lascivious anguish and lowers his eyes to my shoe swaying slowly to the restive quintet. The shadow of his lashes on his cheek obfuscates the sentiment wrung from the drawn cat gut.

My heart is pounding. I am, quite possibly, drowning.

He is catatonic, stunned. He just looks at my shoe, swinging, and thinks of my shoe, and is as tired as I am. He wears the same shirt as yesterday evening. I have on the same shoes.

I remember his lean body, the white forelock and the hair on his chest. I remember the trace of hair down his tummy. I look at his long elegant hands and remember his long elegant penis. I am only half present for he has taken me the night before. I had put on the high heels, arched my back and raced him, stroke for stroke, to the shore. We had beached ourselves.

I hover as he signs C.D's and listens to the enthusiastic compliments. He nods and agrees with all they say.

I sigh and leave the church to the moral admirers who shudder as the wind blows in from my exit.

Chapter Six
Tiziano
The Performer

I have agreed that the day before Tiziano leaves for Boston, will be the last time we have sex, although is plane leaves in the evening today and the late flight would have allowed for a last daytime encounter.

"This way," he says, "our boulder might stay balanced at the top of the hill without rolling back down upon us."

His reason for this "call" is different than mine, but I agree to his imposing a decent ending to the chapter. He says that next time I chose a lover I should not chose a married man with children so that the narrative could unfold openly. I explain that his unavailability had been perfect for my intent. I had wanted to enjoy and understand him as the incredible man I had perceived him to be, without the fear of being possessed. I don't want to be sucked into longing, planning my movements around the possibility of him being my lover or finding himself following a similar pattern for me - not daily or in the long term.

Yes, today, I believe I can follow his wish and we will meet for lunch only. Despite this, my heart tightens at the thought of his beautiful face.

Yesterday, he arrived at my apartment early in the morning. He accepted my bleeding and I felt his fingers, his musical fingers, as I came quickly while he probed me. Once inside me, he stopped, saying he was too excited and didn't want to come yet, but he did. He came quickly, then carefully drew off the bloody condom and cleaned us both up. He wiped his cock with the same attention he gave to his philosophy, a concentrated furrow to his brow.

He came back in the afternoon. I put on my stockings with the seams up the back and the black lacey tops. We stood in the kitchen, him slapping my butt, my "pretty little ass."

"Do you like where I'm touching you?" he whispered with a symphony of strokes.

He rubbed my skull as he entered me. He messed my hair as his palms swirled around on my head. He impaled me on his staff and we moved to my bedroom, my legs wrapped around his waist as he carried me into the cool morning light.

The oval window is recessed deep in the white wall. My long black dress hung by its straps from a hanger covered in white silk. My shoes sat beneath it. In front of the long window, shuttered from the afternoon sun, is a desk covered by a rusty red fraying fabric. The chair for the desk is old and Italian. My pristine drawings lay flat on the cool terrazzo floor. The bedspread is Venetian. The presentation, like a museum, cool, hushed and darker than life, invoked a movie set or a time past.

I watched him throughout. I saved the visual. I formed my body into shapes that would please him. My joints doubled back. My ass was effective. He placed me in poses, adjusted contours. I watched as he came. He turned his head to the side and closed his eyes in a primordial attitude of arrogance. He was transported, self absorbed. His lineage claimed him as he came deep inside me. He was a learned, talented, refined, aristocrat fornicating - a nobleman with a mistress.

We came together. Then he carefully cleaned me with a warm cotton facecloth.

He dressed in his white clothes and sat in the chair. He proposed a last lunch together, tomorrow, on the day he would leave.

Tomorrow has arrived and we look through our sunglasses at each-other's-lover. He smoothes back his white forelock and conducts his words with his long elegant hands. He claims he feels guilty but grateful. He is ashamed of his need. He was aroused by me and couldn't resist. He would like to be a good man so that I would esteem him but he says it as "estimate him." He has entered a path, not in tune with his rationale, an emotional path. This path absorbed energy but also contributed energy. The path didn't eliminate change. Change was encouraged. It enabled the view of a vista of great quality. He says that habit could lessen the quality, that one becomes aware of the performance. This produces a glaring, unflattering light on the path, a light that comes out of the shadows to blind us like sunspots. We must step back and put on sunglasses to see where to go next.

He smiles kindly. "I see you sometimes as childish - this may not be the right word - as naive, innocent. This is not necessarily a bad thing, but you should hold yourself back more often. People take advantage of you, of your energy. You give yourself generously. Don't always be generous. Temper yourself. Build your career carefully. Always believe there is a need for a condom; recognize and act on the need to connect, but stay protected."

We have lunch, only lunch. I interview him. I know I look good to him, but I keep him talking.

Tiziano continues to advise me. "You're like one who's much younger. You could be perceived as one who is in the clouds. Don't allow your energy to be sapped. Allow your philosophy to grow, to change. Reveal less to others than you have to me, for you are hard to resist."

The sex has been a catalyst to render the sex superfluous. Yet the longing remains. I want to touch his shadows.

We had begun unequally for he was the performer, but we had chosen each other. I match his astuteness. He is able to determine my oblivion. Yes, he is a player, but my presence is necessary for him to perform.

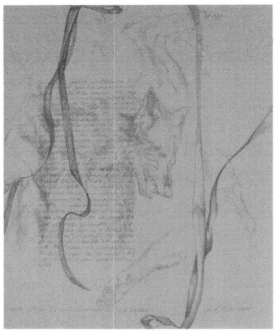

Chapter Seven
Tiziano
Clean Break

Months later, this time in New York, we fall into it calmly, speaking Italian. He is in the city for a concert. I am lying beside him, in my apartment, as I am lying to him. He asks me if I have told my sister, Juliette, whom he met in Venice, about the dream he had of her, the dream where we were all making love together. He had been surprised, on recounting the dream, that I too have entertained the notion. Since our separation I have seen her; Tiziano has not.
I begin, again, lying.

He asks me to be honest.

"Yes, I did tell her."

I confess my indiscretion.

"I told Juliette that you have been my lover. I have told no one else about our liaison. Then, we fantasized...."

We are lying beside each other and I had begun by lying to him. He has to lie, to be here with me.

We develop signals. We begin with propriety, polite and conversational. Then he leans back and I curl up against him and the truth comes out. He begins his lie as we lie down together. My New York apartment is cold. He has entered the apartment, having walked from Grand Central Station, with "*Mio Dio, e freddo!*" Always, when he enters, the weather is with him, on his tongue, in Italian. As we lay beside each other, beside the single pane window, my red shawl isn't warm enough. He turns me over to rub my back warm.

His slight frame is brushed with a perfect configuration of black and white hairs. He's divinely symmetrical, well put together. He smells nice, of skin and hair. He says I am thin and deep. I say he is thin and long.

His movements are those of fencing, clean parries and thrusts. He slaps my ass, my back, my arms and my shoulders with not enough sound to register as a blow. He stuns my surface in order to go deeper. He whispers that he likes my pretty little ass, my pretty little ass-hole. He pins me down with my hands above my head and maximizes my length, the elegance of long and thin. "I like, *mi piace, mi piace*." I watch his face, his neck, his chest, and his symmetry. He is good to look at - *bello guardo.*

He wastes me and doesn't know the meaning of the word "wasted." He spends me, still unsure of the word. He takes me completely. He knows, for he watches me, as I am watching him.

Then he comes noisily, his eyes widening and rolling backwards. He is destroyed and makes a plea for energy and a clean break. I am wasted and he doesn't know the word.

Chapter Eight
Tiziano
Pursuing Themes

He has a reason for being out again this morning and dropping by my apartment, a function to his having left the hotel; he had to buy a newspaper. I thought it was Pravda and the American Cup, but it's football. Sunday, for an Italian, is "football." With the football scores on his lips, he sits, elegant while swinging his leg, his pelvis thrust slightly forward. He registers an innocent delight at the sight of my white running shoes in the line up of black high heels. They are beside the strappy shoes that are his pleasure.

I ask him personal, intimate questions. He reveals himself and again, I am enlightened. He holds himself refined; yet, I can feel his expectancy.

I set him at ease by undoing his shirt.

His underwear is handmade. I know these things for I am his mistress. His aquiline face is still, the hollows familiar. Once again, his pants are at his ankles. His shoes never come off. My panties circle my ankle, a light lacey impediment. He slides down onto the floor. I perceive him as a crumpled black cloth below the white stripe on his head. He breathes on my sex. .Then he rises, and with his pants at his ankles, he hops across my kitchen floor to find a condom.

I know how to receive him. He likes to pursue the same themes although he is curious as to how dirty I am willing to be. He is learning to relax and accept this role that we play together.

He directs me in his language. I am not always able to understand him, but I am panting to learn and will put on my high heels.

Chapter Nine
The Priest
Defrocking

I want to defrock a priest. This Priest, at The Village Church, is a candidate.

His sermon is all about sex with no four-letter words. His choir is made of bouncing, buxom babes with visible cleavages. His hair touches his waist. His fingernails are as long as a mincing mandarin's. He stands in shorts, with a cocky, bad boy stance; his legs bare and tanned as they rise erect from cowboy boots. He speaks of "Daddy" in his sermon, a Methodist minister who has preached in the tents of the deep South. The Priest was well brought up. He is polite.

With his spiritual ardor, he has flipped the ladies, cherished Southern daughters, upside down. He plied them with chamomile tea.

I ask The Priest for a glass of wine to cure the results of the last debauch with Tiziano, an attempt at communion before confession, but the priest only serves tea. I am, therefore, manipulated into drinking his chamomile tea. After church, I walk him back to my apartment and show him my dirty pictures.

He languishes and makes me weaken. He accepts me into the fold and I lick his knees beneath his white frock.

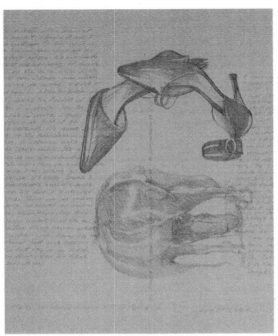

Chapter Ten
Tiziano
A Slight Aberration

In public, when I am at a concert, in his presence, I know that I am his mistress. *He* knows I am his mistress, and we both are aware. We are aware of how I bend, of how he fills in the holes. When I think of how I know him, when we are in public, I think of how he likes to enter me. I imagine the length of his penis. I remember how he looks when he comes. I sense his rhythm and feel if he is under pressure. We shake hands in company and achieve a balance with a slight aberration. The aberration is my presence, his mistress, at a public reception, posing as a distant admirer.

We never brush each other's arm, in passing. We avoid indiscretions. There are no innuendoes, no winks or nudges.

When I open the door to my apartment to let him in, the air bristles. He is barely past the door jam, down the narrow hall and putting his first step on my kitchen floor when he folds around me. He is dressed in his running clothes, still impeccably stylish. Through the loose jogging pants he is hard against my tummy muscles. His length is extraordinary, like a horse in proportion to his body.

He maps my body. He traces over and over the contours with different lines, hard lines, and soft wispy lines. He scratches and etches in lines. He draws signs of desire. He signals his need. We climb the ladder to my hot and sweaty bed. His mouth is absent this time, no foreign words. He looks long and deeply and then splays my haunches like a lamb.

Chapter Eleven
Tucker/Bentley
Aporia/Mouth

Onstage, he plays a bouncer, "Tucker." As the protagonist, he prods the white male lead into romantic action. "Tucker" is big and black. Onstage, he wears black jeans, a Harley T-shirt, a black leather vest and black cowboy boots. He plays cards and swears.

I send a note backstage, signed "the redhead," asking if he and the white male lead will join Blonde Buddy and I for a drink. Blonde Buddy, my friend, is gay and suspects that the white romantic lead may be gay as well.

"Tucker" comes out of the theatre in a long, wool, urbane overcoat. He introduces himself as Bentley. He wears the same black cowboy boots that he had on in the play. He is carrying a gigantic bouquet of white lilies for the ingénue.

Bentley is from L.A. He is in New York for his role in this Off-Broadway play. He is Afro-American, hip and effulgent. At the bar next door, he works the crowd. He strolls between tables. He plugs the show.

"Glad you liked the show! The lead? Tell him that! He needs to hear that." He shakes a hand.

He signs autographs and makes introductions.

"But check it out man. She is hot. Listen to this, man. Listen to this."

The ingénue sings with the Karaoke.

"She *is* hot, man. She's *hot!*" He hands over the ingénue.

Bentley sings "New York, New York" with the Karaoke and dedicates it to "the redhead."

"Are you with him?" He discerns the status of Blonde Buddy, that he is not my boyfriend.

He moves in with, "I like to go to museums."

He is attentive and curious.

Bentley is bed-breaking big. He takes my number.

"I been thinking about you girl. You're a looker. There's a basement bar across from the theatre. Would you like to meet for a drink after the show tonight?"

When he calls, I am studying Italian. I could do with a drink by this time.

He stokes the jukebox with American quarters and, to Hendrix, Cream and The Stones, I tell him the story of my house burning down and my ambition to pursue a Ph.D. At two AM he walks me to the door of 92/94 Sullivan Street.

Now, I can't forget his big fleshy mouth and his kiss the size of an *aporia*. He sucked my lipstick off. It just disappeared. It wasn't on his face. It wasn't smearing round my chin. He showed me how big a kiss could be and how far back it goes. His kisses were corner-less, internal and eternal. His tongue was an organ, as a penis is an organ, more than a muscle. I wanted to hold his tongue in my arms and suckle it like a big fleshy tit.

His penis, the real organ, was big enough to push between us, through all that we were doing with the *aporia* of his mouth. It prodded my ribs and poked the soft of my belly, through the wool of his overcoat, the wolf fur of mine.

I gave in and I sucked and sucked on that big fleshy thing in the darkness.

His tongue, just his tongue, overwhelms my memory and my decency.

In the open, in front of my Manhattan apartment, my white naked mouth sucked his big purple tongue.

Chapter Twelve
Tiziano
Slaps

We spend the New York day together, from lunch until darkness. I meet him at Carnegie Hall after the morning rehearsal and tell him the scary stories he loves to hear from me, stories of the Canadian wilderness.

We lunch in a downstairs café and cancel espressos for a second glass of Italian wine, fearing a small hit of caffeine is "too German." We stride down Broadway together, muffled yet stylish, through the tattered snow.

At 92/94 Sullivan Street, I plug in the string of white Christmas lights and light two small candles beside a bouquet of orange tulips pierced with a single Calla lily.

We talk as the day darkens, relishing the rarity of seeing each other from the morning light to the dusk.

"I like your pussy," he says. "You have beautiful pussy lips but should take better care of your hands and feet."

I ask him what he likes to do sexually and where he draws the line.

"I could take a transvestite, a beautiful woman with a penis," he says.

I know how we will have sex and I tighten. He soothes me. He slaps my arms, my breasts, my ass, my legs. He slaps with honor like a whap at the start of a duel, resounding slaps that raise my chin in defiance. His slaps soothe me. They let him go deep within me.

"Relax," he says. "Relax," and slaps.

My climax is momentous. I die somewhat.

He senses my little death. He stays inside me but flips me over and slaps my cheek, just my cheek. My eyelids spring open. I see his aristocratic face, his eyelids lowered.

"Watch how I am taking you." His eyes ream into mine and I am taken again. I cry out with him and lay destroyed.

"You are destroyed." He reiterates the moment.

The day is gone. Dusk prevails. The room is dim. We have each passed over our boundaries and faint into satiation.

We drink a cup of tea.

He is happy. He tells me the story of his first love, when he was young and shy and rode a Harley in Buffalo. In a sleazy hotel, he had watched her naked shape outlined by the flashing neon light from the tattoo parlor below.

The night is as black as a New York night can come to. It is late and he has left. I climb to my loft bed trying to remember where I have seen a manicure sign.

Chapter Thirteen
The Priest
Drawl

The drawl is what grabs me, so polite and drawn in.

"I am *so* sorry," he says. He says it with cleanliness.

He won't permit me to lift his frock or to play with his collar this time. Instead he swirls his tongued words in my mouth and invites me down the hallway to his bedroom.

It is stark and monastic. He has two pairs of pants and two shirts. He has his vestments for his services. He wears his silver cowboy boots. He has two guitars, an electric and an acoustic. There are no pictures on the walls. Beside the narrow bed is his desk piled with his writings.

He says that he feels guilty, but *he* has led me here. He sings me a psalm and asks to see my magnolias.

Chapter Fourteen
Tucker/Bentley
Lip Smacking Good

I am unsettled. The chance meeting with Bentley, on the street, shines the spotlight on desire and settles it. I want that big black man. His mouth had been so good. He had promised he would be formidable.

"Overwhelm me, Bentley. I will sink low, throw my head back and moan with the flesh."

His mouth had been so juicy it had lapped on my shoreline.

I can sense the wave crashing. Sex will be dark and fleshy and lip smacking good.

Chapter Fifteen
Tiziano
Talking about It has
Made Him Hard

My friend, Penny, the co-founder of "The Nascent Excogitators Fellowship," is visiting my New York apartment and sleeping on my daybed. I have not expected to see Tiziano during this week and am pleased when he calls and arranges a meeting at Starbucks. He is in New York for a photo-shoot and interview with Vanity Fair.

We talk about important things, about him, about me. We discuss the symphony and my toenails and fingernails. We ruminate on his work and he shows me the contact sheet of the recent series of back-lit photographs. The photo of Tiziano, with his bow, mid-stroke on the seventeenth century cello, will support the text of the article. We agree that the photographs are works of art and that the article is utilitarian.

"Do you want to see my toenails?" I ask him.

As we walk our Broadway route, he says he feels we have always done this together, traversed the distance to my apartment, walking home. He is cold and the skin clings to his skull, the headbone that houses his brain, destined for greatness.

At my warm apartment, having shown him my toes, I put on my new green shoes.

"Too pointy," he proclaims. "Italians make the best shoes."

As he uses my bathroom, I call Penny's cell phone and whisper a message. She has a key and is due to arrive.

"Its three thirty, Penny. My lover is here, at the apartment. Give me twenty minutes."

We lie on the daybed. I tell him he has shown me a different side to being a woman, literally, the last time he had taken me. He asks how I liked it and I reply, *"mi piace*, you gave pleasure."

Talking about it has made him hard.

He doesn't want to meet my friend on the stairs.

I lift his shirt and undo his belt. I reach past the white cotton. I touch the soft black hair. I hold his long elegant penis and suck.

Chapter Sixteen
Tiziano
Bianca is Expected in
Fifteen Minutes

I have not seen Tiziano in twenty seven days. I know that there is a symphony tonight and that he is due to arrive midday in the city. He calls from the phone on the corner and asks if I would like him to stop by. Everything is suspended. Bianca is expected in fifteen minutes and their paths must not cross.

I discover again the cotton underwear, the long penis, the delicate stomach and the fragile legs. When the pressure is gone he sits back, but won't deign to rest on my velvet cushion.

Then he stands and begins talking of petty inconsistencies in life. He can't be touched again. We plan our next meeting, tomorrow, before he returns to Boston.

When Bianca buzzes, I hurry downstairs to meet her at the front door while Tiziano waits on the stairs on the next flight up. As Bianca and I make a leggy entrance into the New York taxicab I glance back to see Tiziano leave my apartment building and disappear into the newly falling, furtive, snow.

Chapter Seventeen
An Interlude to Dream

I dream that at a crowded party I meet an entertainer, a singer with black hair and a gray suit of perfect cut. Penny is also at the party. She is talking too loud. I try to keep her in check so she won't tell my secrets. She is name-dropping, bragging about the star whose towel she had used.

Everyone knows and admires the singer. I engage with him, eye to eye. He acknowledges our closeness from the stage, showing the audience that we use the same hand gestures in our careers and public presentations. The crowd disperses. We all go outside the auditorium and he is acknowledged by fans as a great *maestro*.

We walk the streets, displaying our togetherness. He insists, against my mild protests, in taking me sexually, standing up, on the street while people glance at us. I throw caution to the wind. I come. I want him to come as well but he says that it isn't necessary.

This morning, I wake up content. It's Friday, the day I don't have an Italian class. I expect a call from Tiziano. Tonight there is a party we have both been invited to.

He doesn't call, nor does he go to the party.

I cancel Bentley if I am expecting to see Tiziano on the same day. Tiziano, however, has been known to leave my apartment, after sex and without a shower, catch a plane and return home to his wife and children. Yet, he prefers not to be at the same party. We maintain vague notions of integrity.

I lie on my daybed with tea bags on my eyes, listening to Chet Baker. I am in a sublet New York apartment with beige walls and ceilings. The city is buzzing outside. I am miles and miles away from my children and home. I finally have a small amount of time to think.

And it is all right.

Chapter Eighteen
Tucker/Bentley
Cucumber Cream

Bentley has a samurai wrestler's chest. He likes his nipples rubbed and sucked hard. His blackness is spread over sweeping big arms and a big belly. As I pull on his cock it grows big and thick. He bypasses the wine. He rips open my pantyhose. His mouth takes big gulps from my slender sex.

Yes, Bentley is, indeed, an actor. He needs roles and an audience. He likes to be watched.

He issues directives, "Say 'I'm a devil!' Say it again, girl!"

He smells like a cucumber, with cream on his belly and nipples and penis, light-green cucumber cream on a big chocolate man.

He is advancing his career and his ambition overwhelms his perception. He condemns me to sincerity and renders my play-acting useless. I invite him back and he visits me every few days, after performances.

There is a leak and Bentley becomes "Tucker" offstage. The generous host turns into the bouncer. His pugilistic nature seeps into life. I am forced to kick him out of my private club. He messes up my appointments although he has charmed the clientele.

I had just seen Tiziano when Tucker arrived unannounced. He wanted sex. I couldn't change gears that fast. I began to skid. I called a halt. He wanted to keep driving. I asked him to leave. But first, I was made to have sex with him, one more time, like an uncomfortable, backseat screw.

I reached my limits of love and knowledge and could no longer act like an ingénue.

As he lay back, satiated, with creamy cum on his black belly, he booked into Saturday. I denied his wish.

I walked past the fractured reflections in my hallway mirrors, towards the door, while instructing him to clean himself and then leave.

I need the Priest. I feel filthy. I need to confess. I find the Priest and drink a hot, healing brew. We talk sex.

The black bouncer, "Tucker," bounds into the delicate china teahouse with his big black belly still sticky with cum. He whines and complains a viperous tirade at the neglect of his needs. He reiterates that my drawing power was my body and smashes his fist on our tables to make the china cups leap.

"Tucker" has missed the point, lost track of Bentley and broken the rules.

He is banned from the game.

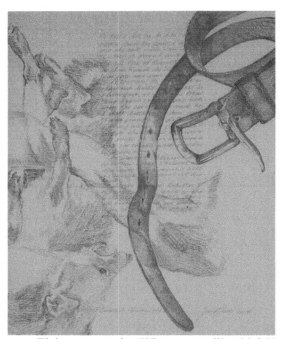

Chapter Nineteen
Tiziano
Cinches the Belt

He'd been to a dinner party and called from a phone booth, late at night. I am reviewing the corrections on my midterm paper and stop in my painful progress through the academic contumely to put on the high-heeled strappy shoes that he likes.

He smells good, his face of cold, his neck of soft fabric and his breath of wine behind peppermint. My body magnetizes him but first we look at my paper. I am emotional at the comments that my professor had penciled in. They are harsh and personal.

Tiziano responds. "Why are you like this? You are a grown woman. You must learn to separate yourself. This is a technical problem."

He is tired, yet animated. He hadn't slept well, worrying about a new musical score. He performed it tonight and received standing ovations for his virtuosity. He is charged with passion.

We fall back from academia onto the day bed by the window with the parking lot below where drunken diners negotiate their exits. We hold onto and squeeze each other; his lean body and my gauzy leopard print dress between his suit and my lack-of-panties. Desire leans on the length of his penis and the probing of his long fingers. The memory of the last time he took me colors the present as his gaze falls down from above me. He is punctuating his penetrating surveillance by removing his clothes. Tailored style slips to floor. He slides his belt out from around his slim waist. The thick black leather has wrinkled the silk of his snow white shirt. It leaves an impression on the skin of his tummy above the hand-sewn waist of the cool cotton underwear.

He feels hot as he lifts my shoulders from the daybed and slides the belt under my neck. He wraps it around and with the deft feel of fingertips slides the strap through the buckle as he bores into my eyes with a stare of concern. He cinches it tighter and tighter as I meet his firm gaze, as my *vague trembling fingers* seek the space between the skin of my neck and black leather. He stops, smiles and plunges his penis deep into me as I grapple the leather encircling my neck. He slaps my ass and my thighs with rhythmic percussion. He begins the litany of desire for my sex, whispers of its beauty and I respond with the cadence of approval at his taste.

He places his cock between the insteps of my shoes so that the spiky high heels dig into his balls with my toes on his abdomen.

He moans "*Le scarpe.*"

He flips me over and folds me back onto myself. He slides off the condom and I suck on the soft skin of his length. I take his balls in my mouth with a juicy vigor. When they are swollen and succulent I whip their damp wrinkles with the end of the belt tongue still cinched on my neck. He comes and cries until the building resounds with the moans of his ecstasy, his pants wrapped around his ankles.

Then he is off in a flash, bemoaning the hour but glad that he's past by my door on the way back from dinner to come on the daybed of his Canadian mistress before boarding a plane for Boston.

Chapter Twenty
Tiziano
A Cozy Day for Bondage

It's April and a blizzard has swept the Sunday Soho streets clean of people - a cozy day for bondage.

Tiziano gathers me up like a baby in his arms I curl up to the length of a three-year-old and yet he squeezes me smaller carrying me in his arms to the daybed.

"Where are your ribbons, master? Tie me up."

"You, child, discovered the esoteric book of Japanese bondage, showed me the pictures and sparked my interest. You must have the ribbons on hand."

I draw out my leopard print scarves, lacey-topped stockings and black velvet ribbons. He works with attention to form and to detail using the ancient illustrations as a guide and a reference. The ties are intricate - drawings on ankles, tattoos on the neck. The knots form patterns, intricate interlacing from my throat to my ankles, my knees to my shoulders. He gags my mouth with a black lace stocking and slips the high heels on my trussed feet.

He slaps and he hits me. He slaps with his belt and digs in with his nails, the manicured nails accustomed to parchment paper and goose quill pens. He rises from this project to place the tawny silk shirt with the smells from his body over my head. The vision of candles dripping on oriental nipples that I had seen in a bondage manual, obscure my reason. I writhe in my prison and cry out as he enters me. He is hurting me and yet I want it harder. Fingers mitigate the onslaught of his thrusts in sync with my pleasure point. Pushed out beyond the thralls of his beauty, he grants the vision of his face as I come, slipping off the blindfold, to blind my anguish with the brilliance of his features.

He watches me orgasm, as I lay on my side with the gag dripping wet. He smiles. He kisses me and unties my feet from my neck and my hands from my knees . He asks permission, "would it be too much for you? Can I take you again?"

I grant permission.

With only my wrists bound by the ribbons causing my arms to encircle his sweet head in the posture of languor, our pelvises become one, pressed close together. He comes, resounds, shudders, cries out again and I watch him, his hollows, his shadows, and his neck, thin and fragile.

He rises to release me. I watch only the long, velvet, soft, supple ribbon as he unties my ties.

He sets free his prisoner.

In the evening dark as he dresses to leave, he asks when I am accustomed to going to bed.

"One o'clock?"

"No. Earlier. I'm usually dreaming by eleven."

Chapter Twenty One
Tiziano
To Continue

Tiziano will be honored with an important prize. He and his wife will also be celebrating their tenth wedding anniversary. They will have a formal service in the Boston cathedral, where there will be extensive media coverage as his wife's family is famous.

Tiziano is worried. He has told me that he is afraid of discovery, that after the ceremony, *all of this* (meaning our affair) would not be able to continue. In the beginning, I had assumed that *not continuing* was the given.

The *continuing* was the surprise, the steadiness of the continuing, the timing of the continuing. Just as I was convinced that it was not going to continue, it has continued. It has continued in the present tense. It has continued not out of duty or to pay for anything, nor for what is expected, but to continue once again.

It is interesting, therefore, this announcement. It takes me by surprise. At the concert, I walk upstairs with the critic and when I return, tipsy, Tiziano is waiting to continue.

My position is that I know *all of this*. The woman, his wife, doesn't know. She may be able to have him by not knowing *all of this*. I may not be able to continue knowing him.

He has done *all of this* with me.

He tells me that the ceremony is in a week's time and that we will not continue seeing each other after this.

I wonder if he is taking me from behind as he is taking her from the front. Or is he taking us both from behind?

Chapter Twenty Two
Dante

There is not just a single sense in this work, "Quercia Stories": it might rather be called polysemous.

There are six subjects that should be asked about any serious work. What is its subject, its form, its agent, its end, the title of the book and the branch of philosophy?

The subject, the whole work then is "sex." The form is "a story."

Allegorically the subject is "a woman exercising her free will," and in doing so, she is earning or becoming liable to the rewards or punishments of justice.

Here continues "Quercia Tales" about a Canadian by birth but not in character. Oakes is the author, in the whole and in the part - it is her sister, Justine, and she is clearly so without.

This branch of philosophy is "eclectic."

The above paraphrasing of the Introduction to Dante's *Inferno* reveals that Justine is not, as Beatrice was for the historical Dante, the muse or the guide. Justine is the subject. In this canto of *Quercia Stories*, Dante is the guide. He leads Justine from emotional slavery into the freedom of non-attachment as the cantina, "Gentle Bondage," continues to unfold.

I have come alone to church, for spiritual healing from The Priest and His Angels. I notice two men being greeted by the Priest. They go to the balcony in order to gain an overview and I follow their lead to safe haven. Soon, they are bookends to my personal presentation - two men, both beautiful. The one to the left is Johnny. The one to the right is Dante with a curl to his lip that makes him a model, an actor, or a movie star.

Dante engages. He is, indeed, an actor, out of work because, he explains - he doesn't audition. There is not enough classical theatre happening and that is where his interest lies, he tells me.

I ask Dante which of the six bouncing Angels is his favorite.

"None of them. They seem too young. The one in the middle is too eager. She has an aura of desperation. The end one has to work too hard to move; she's not in shape. They're too young to really be sexy."

The Priest interrupts his sermon to command the women in the congregation to raise their shirts.

"Show your magnolias!"

"You don't have to do it, 'Beatrice'." The man named "Dante" whispers in my ear.

I would have shown my magnolias, for I'm an avid exhibitionist, but on Dante's suggestion, I demure.

The service ends. Johnny has to go. Dante asks if I'd like to continue into the night with him, to go on a journey. We could go to *Café Wha* or *Pravda* for a drink. I have not drunk all night. I thought that I wouldn't drink for my soul feels pure from the good Priest's words.

But I say, "I would love to go for a drink."

It is I, Justine, that walks down the stairs with the pride of the sanctified space, the choirboy they lusted for, the handsome count of the Gothic cathedral. The Angels hug me, glancing over my shoulder at Dante.

Dante and I run through the snow to a waiting taxicab. In the lowdown back seat of the New York taxi we touch at the knees. He says he is glad he has met his "Beatrice." I am thrilled at having discovered "Dante," a philosopher I had somehow missed in my undergraduate years.

We stop at my apartment. I show him my drawings with the Canadian lover's letters for backgrounds. We decide to rest for a moment, to drink some cool water.

We lounge on my daybed.

Dante quotes Shakespeare, finishing with "a quintessence of dust."

I quote Shakespeare, "to thine own self be true and it shall follow as the night the day," and I paraphrase, "you will get to do whatever you want!"

As we talk, he lays on his stomach by my side, his head at the top of my stocking. He holds my hand and we continue to talk of literature, of art, of the opera. We lounge and we talk and he kisses me. His mouth is slippery and juicy and full of his masculine tongue.

The slight rough of his tongue swirls the inside of my mouth. We kiss for a very long time. He pulls my black Chinese blouse over my head. He undoes my expensive Italian bra, unclips the tiny hooks from the eyes, and lowers me back down with his palm on my back.

He sits back on his heels and unbuttons his shirt. As he removes his T-shirt, he raises his arms and his underarm hair forms a nest for my fingers. He has bronze oval nipples, perfect ellipses on velvety skin. He takes off my high heels looking left, looking right. He peels off my stockings. He slows his pace. He sits at my side, undoes his belt and stands to draw off his jeans, the casual disrobing of a confident young stud. In his white jockey underwear, he asks for a condom and I slip him one from its hiding place under the cushions. He turns me onto my stomach and undoes the zipper of my little red skirt and then he draws off my g-string.

I wander my hands over his skin without a blemish upon it, just the soft firm flesh of a God-like body. I suck on his cock. I vary the motions and rub the head around on my face. He tastes my sex and probes me with his fingers like a man who knows where he comes from. I ask him inside.

He rises up and draws on the condom, hand over hand, on his magnificent penis. He enters me, inch by inch, slowly. I feel the length and circumference of his cock as he slides his slick cylinder in and out. While kissing and kissing, he puts his finger on my asshole. Then he flips me over. He drives from behind. He stops to breathe. He suspends his belief and sucks in more air. I sense his coming, so I let myself go and come with his shuddering sighs on my back.

He gets up. I watch his svelte ass as he crosses my kitchen. He slips off the condom in the dimness of his small journey. I hear the toilet flush away his babies.

When he lays back down beside me, our faces relax as our eyes close together. I hear his teeth click and he startles awake. He looks through his cool eyelashes. He smiles at my smiling. He drifts off. I wonder at the weight of his head on my arm, that I am holding such beauty. I wonder if he is cold, if he will stay the night. I wonder at his unblemished skin.

His eyelids lift. I ask him, "Who were Dante and Beatrice?" He smiles and holds me closer.

It is dawning outside. He rises and begins to dress, apologizing for having to leave so quickly. He starts work at six, moving furniture, a weekend gig only. It is five fourteen. He walks down my narrow hallway cracking the wall mirrors with his electric beauty. He has been a boyish delight, eager to please me. There is no flaw in the evening of fresh-bodied sex. There is no plan to repeat, no need to rehash, no momento to look at. There have been no last names.

Not a trace of him remains; still his image hangs in the atmosphere, the ultimate one nightstand. His stunning beauty will fade from my memory, recalled by Calvin Klein jockey shorts labels.

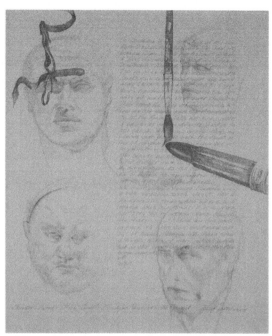

a Mongolian man.

Chapter Twenty Three
The Mongolian
Practiced in the Gambit

At his Chelsea opening, he looks at me. He looks mean and disapproving. He glares at my high heels, my stockings, my waist, my breasts, my shoulders, my hair and is captured by the time he locks on my eyes staring back at him.

He has dark shoulder length hair tied back in a pony tail and the simple solution of a black T-shirt and suit. His work consists of intimidating, large, crystal-clear photographs on hand-made paper.

He gives me his number, writing it on the catalogue.

I have just, for the first time, met

It surprises me to see him at my opening. I walk him through the galleries, introducing him to my friends who find him haughty and intimidating with his gruff Mongolian charm. When he asks to see my drawings I invite him to my apartment.

The evocative letters, hand written in sepia on parchment paper, carry the images of my legs in fishnets and high heels. They sport the torso of David with a bra on his head and the Assumption of the Virgin with her eyes rolled upwards in the direction of a lacey thong. There are crotch shots and lingerie placed side by side with the faint golden glow of parchment sustaining the insinuation of sex.

Blonde Buddy calls to invite us for a drink and in the punctuated arrangements, cutting the titillation, the Mongolian and I avoid an encounter and are pulled back out to the streets.

We meet my friend, Blonde Buddy, in a bar on thirty-sixth street, the Mongolian's choice. A mafia-esque greeting sets the courtesy code. Hands are shaken as I stand by his side in my high heels and good hair cut, one of many women who have stood by the sides of men, not as wives, but as their "ladies," respected and appraised only for their roles in the biographies of the men.

The Mongolian turns a good line. Blond Buddy warms to his tangential personality. The Mongolian puts forth a practical seduction of jocular perusal. He makes scathing arrogant judgments of those who have less than a perfect adherence to style, class and position. He mimics those who are not well feathered or practiced in the gambit. An Asian aristocrat with a long string of pearls and a hundred years of wrinkles, pays her respects. The Mongolian tells me that she has had half of Mongolia's crusty upper echelon as her lovers.

We sip thick rice liquor from shallow bowls. Then, amidst graceful nods and compliments we say goodbye to the venue and Blonde Buddy, and there is "just the two of us." We drop composure and rollick into a taxi uptown. I grant him a visit to his Fifth Avenue apartment. The antique doorman doesn't lift an eyebrow.

His apartment is a modern, vacuous space filled with his large black and white photographs. He possesses an eclectic collection - furniture with barley twist legs, mallets, mirrors and objects whose names are verging on obsolescence. He rolls and smokes a fat joint. We waltz to Asian pop singers. He bends my back with the finesse of a man used to balls and cotillions. He bends me back onto the couch and destroys my lipstick with his great Mongolian mouth. Having no condom, I shield my sex from his dart and he roars like a bear as he shoots his cum, clouded like Mongolian rice wine, over the skin of my soft supple belly.

We laugh at our wildness, then with my head over the edge of the couch and my hair tassling the wood floor, he licks and probes until I come to a climax.

The early morning care of his tawny maid will smooth away the impressions left by a small Canadian body on the Mongolian's black leather couch.

Chapter Twenty Four
Frankie,
A Beat Young Man
From Chicago

The young, black-eyed, black-haired, beat poet Frankie, tells me, while drinking beer at the *Grass Roots Tavern,* that he has had a sexy dream about me. "Oh, you were hot, babe, and there was no age difference. It was just *real good sex.*"

It becomes late at the *Grass Roots Tavern* and there have been many pitchers of beer, bottles of wine and popcorn laced with innuendoes. The air is pure testosterone. I listen to fighting tales as I sit on his knee. Blonde Buddy, who has brought me to this bar, is beginning to waft off topic. He asks me if I'd like to go elsewhere. As I rise to leave, I ask the black eyed, beat boy, Frankie, to join us and sneak away to *The Phallus.*

The Phallus is a small, dark club, crowded with men only. There is no wine. We order Rolling Rock beer and submerge in the warm damp atmosphere of the notorious, heady bar. I twine my bare legs across Frankie's and with an objective eye at the milling minions of maleness, we drink. I ask my black-eyed friend if he would like to visit the back room. In the noise of the voices and the driving disco beat, he answers "why not?" He follows me in the direction of my Blonde Buddy's recent exit.

I lead him by his hand into the dark, bodied blackness of the backroom. I sit on a couch and pull him closer so that he faces me, still standing. I struggle with the tie on his combat pants, find his long erect penis and suck on it until he comes.

Then I lead him, my arm on his shoulder, back to our Rolling Rock beers.

I lay my high-heeled legs across his, once again, and we kiss in the din of the assignations of flirting fairies. They make cursory connections and bathe in the publicity of sex among strangers. I draw back and laugh as my black-eyed friend tells me that he thought I had asked him to accompany me to the "bathroom," not the "backroom," in this club full of gay men.

He *is* game. He's gamey, this black eyed man from Chicago. He has two days of black stubble, rakish black hair, a T-shirt, knapsack and the swagger of the street. It's hot in *The Phallus* with game plans of backroom potentials being dealt out before us. The beer is warm and insipid. Blonde Buddy is still somewhere in the back room.

"Would you like to go there again, babe?" He nods towards the backroom. "Your turn this time?"

We seek the darkness and my place on the couch by the wall. This time he kneels at my feet, puts his fingers up my skirt and draws my g-string to my ankle. Then he begins to lick me.

"You're quite some far-out couple," says a masculine voice to my right.

A strange cock touches my cheek, rubbing head on my skin. I begin to stroke it with my hand, placing the hard penis by my ear.

"Fuck off man, she's mine!" I hear Frankie say from the vicinity of my knees.

To the left, another man squats on the couch. He directs my face with his hand to his cock that he's pumping. When my head turns to the left, with my hand still stroking on the right and the manipulations between my legs from Frankie, I loose my balance and start slipping off the couch. One cock leaves my hand and the other my face. I grapple for my purse as my black lacey thong drops from my ankle to the floor which is grimy on my thigh. I come with panic. The beat boy catches me up and we are out of there, fast, in a scramble. The hands of mystery men clutch the space left clear from our bodies. Cocks are left spraying into the darkness onto Blonde Buddy's shirt.

My black-eyed partner assures me, complicit with our purpose, "I had all holes covered, babe, don't worry."

We pulse with excitement as Blonde Buddy joins us and we go out onto the streets of a staid New York night. But I want my panties back, so we go back into *The Phallus,* into the backroom to grope on the floor. The grabbing begins again. The fingers are poking, trying to push aside cloth covering openings, so we split to the front street, without my thong, and say goodnight to Blonde Buddy.

We walk past the step-ups and step-downs, sexed up and laughing. I am bare-legged, with no panties. His palm is up my slip-dress on my bum. We stop now and again against the brown-stones of the buildings and he presses into me, rubs me.

We pass through a gate in front of an entrance exposed to the street but off of the sidewalk, a covered alcove. People pass by on their way home from movies but we are shades, murky rustlings from a dark recess. His hand burrows under my dress. His cock is out and hard. Heels click by as I squat for the blowjob with my dress at my waist. Protected but public, he then sits at my feet in the down-dirty gutter and licks me and probes with his fingers. With my ass thrust out and my palms pressed on the damp brick, I come. The street hears the moans from somewhere near their soles.

We join the stream of nightlife. At my apartment he tells me I tasted nice. I respond to this blue-collar guy that it is "by the way, nothing I've earned."

We have condoms now. We have sex. His body is small, like Tiziano's, but youthful. He is twenty-seven years old. He is pushed over the edge of reason by my tongue-twirls on his penis. He turns entrepreneur and requests the patent. He dribbles a full glass of water on my backbone. It curls round my ribs, through my thighs to my tummy. As it soaks into the daybed, I come with the dawn.

We climb up the wooden ladder to my bed and a soundless sleep. I go down on his silence as he sleeps. He rouses, then he slackens, a quiet bursting of cum.

We sleep only two hours before we greet the daylight. I don a red g-string and red leopard print T-shirt. We lie on the daybed and listen to Thelonious Monk. I dwell once more on his long slippery penis. He comes sweetly and softly, filling my mouth.

Then he leaves to cool out in Washington Square and I shower to prepare for the walk uptown to a gallery in Chelsea to pick up my slides.

Chapter Twenty Five
Frankie
Booze Bed

The backless strappy dress works well. It's *my* party. I am gay, buzzing and attracting the worker bees to my Queen bee back. The Salsa dancer is at my feet in search of the pollen sticking to my legs from the last flower I've delved into head first looking for the night's perfume.

Down the length of the Bowery loft, Frankie leads an entourage of young and groovy friends. He's shorn his locks and the shiny soft helmet sweeps by me without my acknowledging his wave. In his casual shirt he looks smaller. The whirl of the party is upon me and I don't at first recognize my accomplice from the evening at *The Phallus*.

The Salsa dancer transfixes on the symmetry of my back. The Mongolian gives me flowers and a formal hymn to my sex, a card he has drawn of him chasing my skirts. The blonde man from Amsterdam seeks my sophistication. The Colombian with the long curly hair, tied back with a bright red ribbon, the business man from El Salvador with the muscled arms and the professor who wants to secretly whip me, *all* are by-passed for the beat boy. When I state my preference, he gives up his ride back to Brooklyn in order to continue on with me. He denies his rule of authority, never to spend a second night, and runs his hand over the straps on my bare shivering back as we walk from the Bowery to my apartment in Soho.

Blood is no deterrent. We are barely aloft, stroking smoothly when he comes so quietly it could have been missed but for the milky white semen that slips from the abandoned condom. He grows hard again.

He tells me that he has a girl in Chicago, different from me.

"How so?"

"She's beautiful, like you, but she has black hair, like me. Her figure is full, with big breasts and child bearing hips."

"My hips *have* born children."

"And I have never been with a woman over twenty four years of age."

We wax louder and tell stories, sing songs, duets and singles, and drink wine.

"There's a new boy in town. He's been hanging around. He's the image of youth." I bequeath to him the Stones' song that my ex- husband had believed described his rivals.

"Inside, outside, bedrooms, galleries, everybody knows," he counters with Lou Reed's description of New York.

He keeps me in close. He kisses like glue and pulls my hair. He smokes a cigarette in my bed. He sloshes Chardonnay on my body and drinks from my hollows, then dries my tummy with his tongue and his soft silken head. As we guzzle from the bottle in my booze-bed, he tells a story of his father.

"Dad kidnapped my brother and I. He drove three hours in three days, going from roadside bar to bar, until he stuck with a Marilyn Monroe blonde bartender. Four months with no school, no breakfasts, and a lot of take-out food, perched on bar stools, catching an eyeful, we waited. Mamma, from the awkward position of an assembly line in a glove factory, finally managed to locate us. She came and swooped us all into her beat-up station wagon and brought us back to a proper upbringing. Dad never touched another drop."

Yes, the beat boy from Chicago has stories to tell. He reads Kerouac, listens to Bowie and writes poems on his staple list of "smokes, beer and bread." His head is as soft as a cockatoo's feathers. His sex is silent. I relish my role as his babe in the booze-bed, but the party's over. It's time that he returns home to Chicago, to mamma, his girl and baseball-beat-poetry.

Next morning, we kiss goodbye and I smuggle the quiet cum of the beat young man from Chicago into Canada, in my warm vagina, right under the sniffing surveillance of the border guards. My sophisticated demeanor and educated banter gives them no clue of just how bad I can be.

Chapter Twenty Six
Limits of Love and
Knowledge

I come home to the death of a friend, a woman "known to be difficult." I, however, had known how to relate to her, although she wouldn't allow herself to be completely welcomed, really befriended, by me. She had an intense survival instinct, a need for self-sufficiency. Despite the memory of her abrasive ways, it is hard to come home from New York to the death of a friend. When I look in her plywood coffin, I see that her jaw hangs slack where it should have been tied shut at her death and her eyes are half open, so that I see a clear blue. The women who prepared her body haven't put make-up on her because she hadn't worn make-up when she was living. Flowers cover her body and only her face is visible.

The incidents we shared are all wrapped up now, secluded and closed in her personal history book, her body the casing of the tribute to her life.

I'll miss her wry, exclusive presence. I'm sorry she died so early. She'll miss all the parties, the on-going stories, the theories of "why it's all happening," and "what it all means." She held up a part of the picture.

Mind you, I'm not going to let these same women bury me!

I want my daughter, who is a hairdresser, to cut my hair with a perfect sculpted style and to henna it even a brighter red than the sun gave its glory to. I wear make-up in life. I want my lip liner drawn and filled in with gloss. I want to be absolutely sure that my jaw will be tied shut when I die. I want a manicure and a pedicure. Much as I have enjoyed my body, the way it has looked and the energy it has given me, flowers can cover most of it. But as to what is on under those flowers, if my shoulders are still firm, I would like to wear the Calla lily dress.

Invite my lovers. They have given to me *the limits of love and knowledge.*

Book Two
Lay My Head on the Chest of the Dane

Coons,
oil on canvas, 54"x 42"

Chapter One
The Dane
The First *Jouissance*

Starting with the tips and then the flat of the nail, from the baby finger to the thumb, the left hand first and then the right hand, I put on a first, second and third coat of *vintage wine* nail polish within a faint indigo outline. I am attempting a lady's veneer on my paint-stained-blue fingernails, which should have been roughly scrubbed with a pumice stone for having established an intimate connection with such dirty art. The faint indigo of his Danish irises, framed by the taut skin of his outdoor face, make my eyes sting. I wonder if it is airborne indigo dust that is causing the irritation. I can't see the top of his head, under cover of his backward hat above the Viking brow, nor can I see his teeth fully. I see only the teeth, white and straight, on the right side of his mouth as his lip curls up to talk or smile. His voice moves up and down more than his lips with a Danish lilt that sounds like a voice in a kilt when I try to imitate it.

He tells me a story of leaving his one-month-old baby girl to return to Canada to work. The story lasts through wine and dinner and the ride in his fifty-six Willys with a speaker phone from a New York taxicab hanging from the dashboard. The dialogue circles repeatedly back to sex and we include each other in our privileged perspectives of single travelers through lust.

He drives and he parks and we kiss and drive and park and kiss until too much is showing for the lit city streets. So, at the top of a hill we pull off, a *real* country drive-in, and with the lights of the city spread below and beyond us, from a height filled with fresh country air between the old Willys and the pristine homes, we feel each other up. We neck. He is careful, the Dane, until he comes in my hand, his cum clouding the shine of my *vintage wine* polish.

He confesses that he had thought of this as he'd seen me stand on a ladder in my gallery. With his soft Danish lilt he deems me "wild" as we rumble down the old logging road to the picture book possibilities below.

Chapter Two
Manuel
Salsa Headstand

The Dane had come in Canada, a cupful in my hand, stored and released. I had left him suspended on the hillside of my hometown, unsure of what I'd done, but accustomed to the ease with which I had done it. I return to New York for six days. I alight briefly with Manuel, one night only, as I continue my inquiry into the limits of love and knowledge.

Manuel and I had danced salsa at the first party and I had seen his bronze built arms beneath his light blue cotton shirtsleeves. His hair is black. His eyes are blue. He's a Spanish speaking man from El Salvador, a financial consultant who saw my red leopard skin g-string panties and my black lacey topped stockings when I stood on my head at the second party. He's grown a trumpeter's fringe for the third party, a small black tuft of hair below his lip. We dance and his ex-wife, the long legged, red lipped salsa dancer shows me new steps and then leaves. He stays. He's seen my panties and he stays for me. At the close of this party his hand follows the silk velvet of my dress, over my hips, between the g -string's edge and the stocking tops. He has a car and offers to drive me home.

We careen up the four flights to my Manhattan apartment and fall onto each other on the couch, three parties away from our first having met. He pulls the black velvet dress over my head past the gold Egyptian necklace. He draws the Venetian red panties down over my legs with the lacey black stocking tops.

He unhooks the Venetian red bra and tells me, "*Carina, carina,* we are people of passion. I live for this passion."

I grip his hard eager cock with my hand, then with my sex. I grip with my muscles clutching the up-stokes.

He turns, flips and strokes me from all directions. He speaks little love names in Spanish and comes with *"carina, carina, carina!"*

He pleasures me.

The night has been unabashedly soaked in wine and the juicy passion of our two fit bodies. We have accepted our license to respond to our lust. We are free and wild and abandon everything but the clichés that stick to the senses.

The morning is quiet and I hold his cock until it hardens and he calls me *"carina,"* continues to stroke me and then abandons the condom and comes on my neck with a sweet almond lotion.

Then it is seven AM and they tow cars in New York City as the dawn drives the workers to work and the street-cleaners to clean. He takes my card with him and rejoins the city and the thousands of bodies in business.

The trace of his departure is fading, bleaching under the morning sunlight, as I leave my New York apartment to return to the indigo eyes of The Dane.

Chapter Three
The Dane
A Private Parade

"Shut up!" I command my 'minpin' who is nipping at The Dane's heels. I ask The Dane if he would like a glass of wine and to bring me one to my bath, "please."

I lay on my back in the wine colored bathtub with gold lion claws and cross my hands across my breasts with my leg demurely tipped to the inside of the bathtub. He sits at the end of my tub on a chair with a curl of pubic hair showing through the clear vinyl covering the seat cushion. He explains in detail that the hose on his Willys jeep had burst and is spurting oil like an open wound on a dying horse. I rise from the tub as my miniature Doberman attacks his feet again.

I dry off my body and go to my red bedroom to put on my lime lacey bra and g-string panties. He watches my private parade as I go from the drawers to the closet to the bed. He tells me I have the body of a seventeen-year-old so I draw him down on top of me. I pull his shaved head closer, his bronze face, his strong Viking body with all of his clothes on, a blonde turtleneck sweater and jacket and his boots bitten by Bonita. We kiss on my bed as he slips past the g-string with his mouth adept and his tongue energetic. His fingers play and probe. He draws back to take off his jacket and sweater.

For just a moment he looks like Picasso in a blue striped T-shirt.

His chest and his arms are packed hard with muscle, tattooed very black on his fair Danish skin. Being a body builder, he's shaved as smooth as the top of his head, which he'd shown me, newly shaved, as he sat at the end of my bath. He's smooth like his cock, which has a wide hook when erect. Only his balls, tight, are dusted with blonde Nordic hair.

My legs wrap around his packed Danish muscle, his breadth and solidity. I follow the curve of his cock with my mouth. His masculine strength finds its way past the lime lace. His golden beauty, like the Egyptian gold on my neck, encircles me. He welcomes me home, back from New York, with a deep Danish lilt. He pulls me up on his lap like Siva with Sakti. The strength of his torso protects as he kisses me and cups my pink slim with his packed body. With no need to ask, "when?" he takes me and I cry out a chorus.

We roll onto our backs with our heads over the bedside, the blood flowing back from our bodies to our brains. His face is composed and his blue eyes more distant - the Dane, the first time in the red sheets of my bed.

Chapter Four
The Dane
The Taste of His Fruit

I had believed that "exotic" was southern in origin, twisted lizards or *emozione* on a hot Latin night. Now the exotic is Northern, brought from a distance by a sailor whose tattoo laden arms tell stories of "Harald the Blue Tooth" and carpenter guilds. The Dane builds log structures with the strength of his chest and his massive arms.

He wears a gold earring bought in Bangkok. He rides a dirt bike as he did on the sands of Australia in a jacket that he left in a bus in New Orleans and retrieved the next day to stop the sun from spreading his brand new tattoo.

He's lusty and warmed up, pours the cock like a pirate whose private pillage is his birthright. He knows that the taste of his fruit is exotic far beyond the shores of his framed northern homeland.

He's a traveler who has left a new born babe, the offspring of a bitter relationship, in her cradle of wood in Denmark. His grief for her touch is breaking as he tells me jokes of beached whales. Still, he misses his first born and holds out his hands with the cup of his palm on her invisible head to show me the length of her wee-baby body. He's a month from her birth and the sound of her cries. Half a globe away, is her mother who carried that part of him present, to keep him more present, to tie him to her and his homeland.

Yes, he's missing his baby, but he's regaining his land legs as he lies under red sheets with my fine pubic hair framing his half-frozen smile. While in Denmark, baby sleeps peacefully. She knows that her daddy will return and reclaim her to show her new seashores and log homes.

Chapter Five
Byshe
An Interlude on the
Side of a Poet

I am running a bath for The Dane when I hear the crunch of gravel in the driveway below the bathroom window. I look down on the creamy hood of an antique Morgan.

I come to the door, flushed, phone in hand to meet the poet, Byshe, a little flushed.

He vibrates and greets me with "Hi, Sugar."

He says he is driving in the neighborhood and wonders what I am doing.

I am obliged to answer that I am getting ready to go out with the Dane, that I am running his bath.

The poet emanates beauty. He has fair skin, tight shiny black hair and a goatee. He is wearing a V-neck sweater. He solicits desire. He draws my desire through the screen mesh where it sticks on his body and the gleaming Morgan.

He promises me glamour.

I've read his sexy poems. I've seen the paintings that are tattooed on his arm and back.

I'm waiting to even kiss him.

Chapter Six
The Dane
Vikings Walked Out

I have run the Dane's hot bath and put on a Harlow-style slip. I come from upstairs to meet him at the front door so that the bias- cut satin will float above my knees from the updraft of my descent.

As he bathes, I sit at the end of my wine tub on the chair with the curl of pubic hair, where he (and other lovers) had sat to watch *me* bathe. I have the long leisure privilege of staring at his body.

As the Dane bathes he describes he word "Viking."

"The Vikings walked out. The Vikings went off." His brow furrows at the thought.

He presses his muscles to the walls of the big clawed tub and moves his body as he speaks. He tests his back for aches and pains, rolling his shoulders and stretching his arms. He glistens. With his strong hands, he circles his ankles, his back rising out of the water - an island of muscle. He slides his hip on the warm enamel and rolls onto his side with his knees to his chest and the calloused bottoms of his wandering feet pressed to the white enamel. He curls up like a fetus, his back soothed by the hot vanilla oil I have used to scent his bath. He passes the palms of his Danish hands over his shaved head. His penis lolls. His tattoo soaks to blacker. Slowly, continuously and sinuously, he poses his body in positions of redemption.

He is deep in his head with this turning and testing, turning the pages in old Danish history books. The tools tattooed on his forearm pulse with his heartbeat as the red wine and hot water relax his propulsion. He takes stock of his strength and then he stands. The cascading drops cool his back in the breeze. The blonde body hairs perk up. He raises his thigh to straddle the enamel roll of the tub and soon arrives on dry land, on the shore of my red bedroom.

On the red bed he defeats my wrestling and plunges deep in my sex. I come quickly, unable to stop the ascent of emotions as he strokes, doing push-ups with a sweet smile on his face. He squishes and squelches and pumps into me, fast and furious, slow and sensuous.

The Viking has walked out. He is immersed in a new land and exploring the depths.

He is tapping his way with his blind cane to glory.

He is giving to me what he should have been giving his wife.

Chapter Seven
The Dane
Pillaged by a Pirate

He strides through the front door of my gallery, down the runway set for tomorrow's fashion show, through the trace of scents left by the models. The heads of the designers turn towards him causing a lull in their projections. Striking, he comes towards me, hot and bothered. We leave for a bar.

He reiterates his pathetic position, his longing for the baby he'd left behind in Denmark. I pull on his teeth, gauging the strength of his gums but they keep a tenacious hold and continue to ache. He whines and complains that he is whining.

Doubt curls around me finding crevices to lurk and lodge. He insists that it is not the mother for whom he is pining. She has poked him in his soft underbelly. She has staked him with this birth, planted a flag of connivance on his far native soil. She has ignored his position and supplanted his claim. He now feels shut out of his home where the life he'd created is sheltered by Denmark's old family ties.

At the bar, his blue eyes dart around beyond my right shoulder. When the long legged waitress stops interrupting, I risk an intrusion into our unspoken future.

"If the Danes will permit you to bring back the baby, I will help you. That's all."

He accepts with no plans to do groceries.

He's been watching a young woman beyond my right shoulder. She comes over and they chat. She explains to me that she's known him for many years - that he comes and goes.

He tells her that I know this too.

He tells me, "She's a clerk at the grocery store."

We leave the bar and he drives me to pick up my car. He thinks that he is too tired to come over but I promise not to detain him. He will gas up the Willys first and then drop by for a moment.

In my bathroom, I look in the mirror as I redo my lipstick. My face is familiar but appears tired in the night-light. I wondered if he will come over or if I have pushed him too hard: he may just drive home to sleep. He could call me the next morning, I would accept it.

The Willies pulls up. He is there in the porch light with a soft salutation.

In the warmth of the red room I straddle his ass. I massage his strong back. My tiny hands hurt him.

It is the bulk of his chest that impresses me and the blonde downy hairs that cover the mounds. His body is divided into segments of muscle. His cock has soft shiny skin when it's hard and hooks like the Captain's lost hand.

He jerks off on my tummy, slow and steady, rubbing his cum on me. He sticks two fingers into me and with bird cries of pleasure I screech like a parrot for the pirate of Penzance.

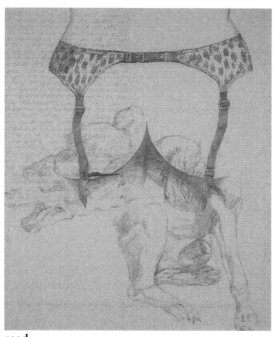

Chapter Eight
The Dane
Backseat Driver

When The Dane was a little boy, riding in the back seat of the car with his brother, his father would pull off to the side of the road with a jolting jerk. He would sit for a moment with his forehead resting on the back of his hands, leaning on the steering wheel, despairing. Then an idea would come to him and he would turn to the brothers and say, "Push boys! On the back of the seat! I need your help. Let's get this car back on the road." The little boys would push on the leather in front of them as the car fired up once again and continued on down the Danish road.

The Dane tells me the story, tenderly. He has sworn to himself that he will not leave his children behind for work, as his father had left him and his brothers and sister. His father left them for a piano bench in his restaurant in Copenhagen, a piano bench left warm by Thelonious Monk, Mingus and Eroll Garner.

Yet for the Dane, too, his work is foremost. Swearing and cursing drive him, seemingly angry at the challenge of the formation of a hand-hewn edifice. His work is physically difficult. It defies inertia. It renders gravity a liar. He butts his head bald. He grits his teeth. He grunts and curses "the other" as he lifts the long timbers one round higher. He shaves off the excess to a perfect line with an ancient adze, as precise as the strength of one man's arms can manage. This warm-up of reduction will suck the top log closer to the one below it but barely makes a difference to the great weight of the timber. Only by cursing ("the bitch, the cunt, the mother fucker!") will he be able to raise the weight and position the timber. Then he steps back, a man. He's had "the bitch" and repositioned "the other" in *his* image through the strength of his body and his tenacious will.

The work consumes his life and his time. The timbers have him "pussy-whipped." They were the cause of his leaving his new tiny daughter, whose warm fragile head he's missing right now. The timbers are also the hard road, back home to his daughter.

He curses, still, as he drives to my house. He steps down from the Willies. He stops swearing.

He comes to my door, late from his labor. He breathes, steps through the portal and in the soft light, I raise my glass to him.

I drink from a hand blown wineglass. It's lime green at the top with swirls running round its five-inch height like a tress of hair that has fallen on a damp cone. The stem is the color of the flesh of a cantaloupe laced with russet. The red wine sits like a garnet in the globe.

The Dane's eyes are glistening azure from his tanned face. The blonde fuzz on his chin is determining the nascent shape of a hipster's beard. I present him with a hand blown goblet, which he can use to drink from while we are drinking together. When he leaves, the glass will stay behind for the next lover. He lifts the smoky glass bowl with his work stained fingers on the golden stem, to his half-frozen smile.

"*Skol*! May we drink like this forever."

"Do you think so?" *I* am the doubter.

"I *know* so."

He swirls our evening around in his mouth. He tastes my small breasts, my slim legs and the tuft of hair on my pubis, which was first spied as a hillock through my cranberry dress. We sit on the back porch; his bronze legs a rest for my white feet with their crosshatched impression of the straps of my abandoned high heels. He tells me not to move my feet from his legs. He says that I am perfect, just as I am.

"In Denmark, it is said that a woman is like a glass of clear water which quenches a healthy thirst. You are a sparkling, fruity drink from an exotic country carrying the taste of a free foreign land. The rich swelling of ripeness reopens my taste buds to your knowledge and pleasure. I want to drink more."

In my red room I lay on top of him and we kiss great gulps of each other. He has become more muscular. His virility is packed tighter. I linger on his belly before I touch my lips to his penis that reaches right to the open waist of his shorts, the tongue of his belt flopping limp to one side. I suck on his cock.

He enters me and we swivel around our joined genitals. He strokes, handles, turns my body and rotates me. He raises me up and down with his immense arms as he stands at the end of the bed, never leaving me, deep, deep inside me, raising and lowering my sex on his cock. He lays me back on the bed like a baby lowered into her cot. He muffles his face in my fur. He says that he is almost too tired to cum. He slides me along the red sheet, still inside me.

Then he reverses, pulls out and splashes my belly and thigh with his cum. I come with his excitement. I quiver. The tuft of my pubic hair is damp as his cum dribbles onto the red sheets. I tremble and coo with the wonder of pulling apart as we came together.

The Dane is re-energized.

"I'm about to break free, to go wild," he declares. "I am going to let my goatee grow long and then braid it in order to tickle the lips of your pussy. The Viking's here, baby! My sword is sharpened and I'm going to use it. I'm in the driver's seat now."

Chapter Nine
Tiziano
Baroque Interlude

Tiziano calls from abroad. He has been performing in a concerto for the royal house of Austria. It is one in the morning and sufficiently private for him to be able to call me. He is dropping in from his baroque and heavenly perspective to assure me that he is a different kind of a Catholic. He is my lover.

I urge him to come. The sound of my voice has given him an erection. Somewhere in Austria, a sink overflows with Tiziano's sperm as he watches the hollows of his face in the bathroom mirror.

Although I am remaining outside of the family circle, I am the dynamic that ensures the circle is not broken but joins upon itself, with no point a beginning or an end. I am the mistress, the lover, without bearing the child, falling in love, or having to believe in order to continue. My record-taking demonstrates the detachment, the desire to lift out of immersion and create an empirical method, which will illuminate the chemistry of attraction.

My lovers know that I won't fall in love with them. I don't believe in the concept. The pressure of consistency is alleviated when immediacy consumes guilt. There is no need to impose an order. There is no expectation of a future and no waste from the past. All that exists is contained within the room with the blinds pulled down, the curtains drawn, the doors locked. Under the covers, undercover for the other, the skin of one body touches the skin of the other body, untranslatable, except as warm and present.

As the lovers drop into my life, cross-pollination permits me to bloom. And they become men again, making honey.

Chapter Ten
The Dane
Undercover Dancer

On my deck, overlooking the backyard, the Dane dances round his nemesis - his baby and his perception that we must remain secret as lovers. Her mother may bring the baby to Canada. He asks me if I would feel uncomfortable if she came over with the baby?

I assure him that the first night in his Willys, I had granted a hand job, not in-spite-of but because-of the story he'd told me. It was an act of compliance.

I tell him, "I can accommodate your situation. You're a European man with a one-month-old baby. I'm simply your mistress in Canada. It sits well with me, honestly. I don't want to buy groceries."

For when I lay my head on the chest of the Dane, I hear his heartbeat. I find solace not in the protection and potential for battle in his muscular chest, but in the diversion of his heartbeat. I listen to his heart beating and my cares *fold their tents like the Arabs and as silently steal away*. I am consumed by his heartbeat. The loud throb bristles with static and interrupts my wiles and ways.

Further more, his elaborate eloquence flips off his lips, passes through my benign receptacle and comes out a story. To the question "Am I seeing him?" - I answer with a summer story. He is, without opposition, the author. My license to relate is secured by the origin. His reel unwinds and I record.

He is attentive to detail, "by noon the temperature was upward of 45 degrees centigrade...."

He tells me how he poured the black sweat from out of his work boots and worked on the soles of his vulnerable cracked feet. Blisters broke out on his chest from the sun. His body was slippery, oiled and dusted by sawdust and wood chips. The wind was annoying, blowing dust so that his eye wept red as the chips skimmed his iris. He slit a vein on the top of his foot with his adze but blood went unnoticed as he traveled from gravel to timber to truck. He swallowed and pissed out four gallons of water. His back forfeited a future year.

He'd drawn up a budget for half the square footage, a monk with a plan to house the spirit of his God. He revised it and topped it off with a gift - he would adze the roof trusses, which would glow like a cathedral roof, blessing his labor.

Today, he has worked with the silence of his adze, his axe and his chisel. The building site is on a golf course. He has danced on the velvet green stage for the women passing in golf carts, whose men have wrinkly knees. The Dane is at work, away from his baby, performing his life with his magnificent body, a body that inspires ladies to have babies, a burst of babies for timber frame homes.

But if he had heard the wrong dumb question asked just one more time, he tells me, he would have raised his axe or sliced a shin with his adze. As it is, he defended his obsessed vision by hurling his axe where it stuck in the wall above the golf cart careening beyond it.

At the end of the light, he sharpened his tools, washed his clothes and bought bananas. He wrote his letters. He left himself the time to stop by on my back-porch, with a long string of metaphors. They end with "a sword that is sharpened, ready for use." They began with "a pail to piss in." They passed through "a friar with a passion for God" and then through "Excalibur" to reverberate with a tuning fork tone.

His pain is inspired. It has the vengeance of angels. His distance from his baby causes him more heartache, more heartbeats than makes the night ready for sleep. The gallons of water he drank at the work-site flowed out the corners of his eyes when the shade hid his tears.

Like the biblical Mary, the one who washed Jesus' feet, I'm diminished by a doubt that I may not be worthy of trust from this inspired Viking. If it was possible to say we were lovers in the open, would I want to admit to this love affair?

He's damaged.

His nail gun is loaded with six-inch apocalyptic spikes. Mentally, he holds it to his temple and jumps from the airplane. He pulls on the ripcord; the shoot won't open. Free-falling through crystal clear blue space he plunges towards the green earth below. When superman's an asshole, he tells me, he tempts brave beings to jump, to test their drunken fate. But the tempted Dane jumps and his head stays intact. It doesn't smash open.

But his back is bent double as he approaches my body. And his touch is inclusive. I qualify as an acolyte, but I'm not drunk enough to jump.

I am brought to my knees by the ardor of his pain. I join him where he lies on his back on the earth. My ear brushes the hairs on his chest as I lie here. I listen to his heartbeat.

He's a Dane. He is damaged.

He's dawning. He is game.

From the dead end of my bleeding I open my legs. He can come inside and learn to accept the petty theft of his child.

The gathering of food will remain outside of logistics. He will do his shopping. I will do mine. I grant permission to piss in my bathtub. We both know that urine will make the skin shine.

He rambles on, eloquently. "We let our horses graze in the fields of the sublime. The adrenaline between our legs begins above the clouds that hide the peak of the mountain, beyond our comprehension. Our steeds were born from the cowlick on the crown of a colossus who lumbered into view and astounded the shepherds. We mount and ride through the crops of our time. The scythes in our hands cut a swathe for the media and expose all the cynics that are bred in this land; this land that is designated free range, Justine, commonage for the people."

His visionary prose cuts through my allusions. Legs open and close like scissors in the Dane's hand.

And the Dane is under the covers, between the red sheets by the time I return from locking the doors and taking the call that announces that my son will be at the movies. We will have time.

I take his photo, trick him into taking off his shirt and showing me his muscles. He throws back his head and pounces about my room with his arms raised high in a languid, pop-star mode. I could nestle the top of my head in the generous curve of his armpit. His pectorals meet the back muscles as they round his rib-cage, creamy and white where the sun hasn't brushed color, a dark flight pattern of hair where the sun hasn't bleached. He's a natural exhibitionist, with the hip-swinging, dick-twirling vitality of a stripper.

I get a good picture.

I'd had a good look through the lens of my camera so I know what is lying under my red sheets. I draw down the cool cotton to see his firm bronze belly, and find his silken penis curving, resting on his abdomen. The muscles turn in from his thighs to meet a crease and then testicles, golden-downed balls.

His virile contrast has me acting like a dame who's a looker, a hooker, and a broad. I lie on my hip and stretch my leg above my head, feeling my bum cheeks framing the g-string. I place his hand on my ass and pump him up hard.

I am bleating as he takes me, a lamb lying limpid.

Then he really goes at it. He pumps and he thrusts, rhythmic push-ups enlarging his muscles. He drips sweat on my breasts. He comes on the lace of my bra and my belly. He makes my g-string sticky.

We rise from the red sheets. In the light from the hall, for an invisible audience outside my door, he grinds and swerves so his dick bounces and whirls like tasseled boobies.

Chapter Eleven
An Interlude of Conscience, Morals and Ethics

A work of art organizes and articulates understanding of experience. Do "ethics" attach themselves to the work of art or to the experience from which the articulation comes?
If sex with another is used as the research for art in order to illuminate the questions of life, where does morality belong - to the sexual experience or the artwork?
The question arises as I continue my research into the limits of love and knowledge and find myself entering a realm of confidence with a sexual partner. Time and repetition has created a private bond with The Dane.

Heidegger wrote an essay on technology when the Nazis were in power in Germany. He held the prestigious and influential position of head of the National University and he was exploring an idea he termed "the standing reserve":

When destiny reigns in the mode of enframing it is the supreme danger. The danger attests itself to us in two ways. As soon as what is unconcealed no longer concerns man, even as object the one so threatened exalts himself and postures as the lord of the earth. In this way the illusion comes to prevail that everything man encounters exists only in so far as it is his construct. But exclusively, as standing reserve and man in the midst of objectlessness, is nothing but the orderer of the standing, then he comes to the brink of a precipitous fall: that is he comes to the point where he himself will be taken as standing reserve.

Within Nazi philosophy people were considered "standing reserve." Jews were killed for not feeding into the idea of progress put forth by the party. They were not a viable resource to be maintained in the standing reserve. The Nazis were posturing as lords of the earth.

The writer or artist who feeds "life experience" into the creation of the artwork uses this experience as a "standing reserve." When the standing reserve consists of the intimate conjoining of the artist with a sexual partner, then moral and ethical questions arise.

When *the tents of the day have been folded* and *I am stealing away home*, ordering creeps in. The events of the day are placed in my hands to be turned, as the divine creator whose position I assume, into "art." My raw material is my engagement in society and, being engaged, I am a part of the raw material. Just as my ordering of this standing reserve is destined by me, I, as a part of it, am destined and thus lost to it. From the freedom of non-existence, as I bring the work of art into existence, it enters the realm where it is now free for the taking - a 'free for all." I can be judged through this work of art.

My calling is to create art. I live to experience, with this end in mind. I anticipate the experience I am living as part of the standing reserve and am myself a part of that future picture. The creation of the work also becomes part of a standing reserve for the next wave in the future. Where is the ethical responsibility in this cycle?

When I have sex with the Dane, anticipating the engagement as standing reserve or art fodder, and assuming the omnipotent stance during the experience (which does not cancel emotional immersion, enjoyment, and sexiness), I lend both him and myself to destiny. We are not just two people having sex, but a resource material to be used in the future. If the ethical relationship is to the experience, to the private act of intimacy, then to retain the integrity of intimacy it should stay as pure now-ness. To transfer the intimacy to the standing reserve to be used in the future as art places the intimate act in another arena - from the bedroom to the board room, from the boardroom to the gallery. The standing reserve takes me from the private bedroom to the public gallery and my partner along with me.

The art object, in this instance, is this book, which is also placed in a visual context as cursive writing on drawings. The truth of the artwork could justify the sacrifice of the intimacy, of the other, of me and of my reputation. At this point the public looks at the work and reads it. It can be digested and contribute to *their* standing reserve.

Does this reveal anything or just add to confusion?

Sex and morality can also be submitted to this ordering. The development of a moral code is founded on precedents. Sexual intimacy, when totally private and enacted with no record taken, doesn't enter the standing reserve. Sexual intimacy used as a resource for knowledge, as it is ordered, documented and processed - destines. To communicate outwards, to make public the two way communication of sex, changes the status of the sex act from object to standing reserve. Conversely, to remain moral to the act itself within our present guidelines, our destiny is to remain silent, private, and intimate.

I have arrived at a point with the Dane where it no longer appears to be ethical or moral to use our story of intimacy as a path to destining. The precedent has now been set. The circumstances I have related in the stories have become the status quo. They have become events that, through usage, examination and record-taking, no longer have to be turned over and probed and poked at. The challenge now is to maintain. Specific cases will demand my attention, where I will be obliged to write, to order, to place within the standing reserve and destine. I may need to conduct a full-scale discovery if the status quo is contested.

Heidegger's precipice is not dark for it has been illuminated by history. Heidegger, with his interpretation of the standing reserve, was branded a Nazi. In the Nazi's omnipotent inquiry, Jews became a raw material in the standing reserve of statehood. The quest for humanity, morality and ethics was distorted and the ensuing destiny was profound.

To impose an analogy to Nazism on my inquiry into the limits of love and knowledge is extreme. Still, in an inquiry into intimacy, people are burned and hearts are exterminated. The risk of creating becomes immense. Repetition, mass production, the possibility of pollution, all components of publication, constitute the elements of risk.

There is now, more than a fresh examination, a repetition in the writings concerning the Dane. This repetition has become a building component. The plans have passed the building inspector. The foundation has been laid. The plumbing is working, drains are draining, air vents installed. The wiring is laced through the framework, the electricity's on, and lights are burning and illuminating the actions. The heat's on. The house is clean. The paintings are hung. It's time to dwell in this destiny.

Chapter Twelve
The *First* Dane
The Status Quo

The *first* Dane contests the status quo.

The present Dane is the *second* Dane to become a research subject in the quest for the limits of love and knowledge.

The *first* Dane is the man I married, my ex-husband, another pirate, another Viking. He is present only in my dreams for, presently, he loathes me. He wrote: "A waist of 23 years and 1.2 mil and for what?" Ever a poor speller, he had meant "waste" not "waist." The petite circle of my waist is, indeed, one of my prides. Today, as I finally brave being on his property to move my possessions out of my studio, I discovered that he has covered my country studio walls with a display not unlike the *Degenerate Art Exhibition* staged by the Nazis. Inept, black felt-penned slogans of malificence were juxtaposed with my paintings and photographs.

Following our divorce, he had retreated into the seclusion of an insulated resentment and disappeared from the physical framework of my life. His scrawled reappearance makes me realize that it is impossible to dwell in this destiny, that the paintings that are hanging are actually covering holes in the walls. The status quo has been contested and I must write again.

Thus I continue my research into the limits of love and knowledge and document with gusto!

Chapter Thirteen
The Dane
A Sense of Smell

I awaken panicked, like a high-strung sketchy mare smelling a storm crackling on the far hills. I stop and go, move, then hesitate. This panic, unlike fear, is not determined. Panic derived from fear knows an adversary. The eyes squint to focus on the path forward. The body becomes tensile, ready to defend, to do battle. But undetermined fear doesn't hold a position. Physical space becomes a boundless possibility. There are no doors to exit by. There are no corners to hide in.

The maleness of the *second* Dane's workspace sets me at ease. The walls of the log cabin have grown higher, forming a surround of golden wood. From the end of the building, the empty window frames look onto clean golf greens. The woods twinkle in the late afternoon sunlight through the lateral vistas. The cabin is at the intersection between wilderness and manicured greens.

The Dane has been thinking of me. He likes the way I smell.

He has spent two days with the blacksmith and they have installed a ridgepole. Twelve feet below, on the floor of the basement, a greasy hole forms the female socket into which the upright male is sunk. A life-size Leonardo Da Vinci's "Man," hands and feet touching the rims of his circle, would describe the size of this female orifice. The golden male swivels deep in the darkness when the Dane turns the wooden peg from the captain's post above. There's an iron bracket a step up the ridge pole from which extends a boom, like a cock emerging from another erect cock. The boom will assist in the placement of the next set of rounds on the walls. No longer will the Dane heft the heavy timbers, above his knees, above his chest, with the strength of his back and his thighs bulging with the strain of lifting. The medieval ingenuity, rigged for balance to the "deadmen" in the four corners of the basement, will swing the logs high until the touch of The Dane changes their direction with the lightest pressure of his fore finger.

My panic recedes into the thick viscous smell of resin. Anxiety relinquishes control of the territory, backing off into the shadows, into the woods.

The Dane's eyes follow the line of my body, from my face to my feet, over the contours of my breasts, my firm tummy, and rest on the outline of the tiny bow from the top of my panties which forms a relief on the surface of the fabric of my dress. His hand is on his axe, resting, head down, at his side.

With the back tip of his left hand, he pushes gently on my shoulder to brush me aside. He looks past my breasts to the window space behind.

"See that?" he says as he points at the sentinel tree in the distance.

Lifting it with his right hand in a curve back past his hip and then up over his shoulder, he hurls the axe out over the golf path beyond and THWACK! It embeds its head in the tree.

The advance guard of shadows retreat with their compatriots. Sunlight and strength scream a victory "yawp!"

We plan a trip to the island. He will call in the morning. Some day, he tells me, he will have me in the cool of the basement tied up to the ridgepole.

He smells me again.

The next morning there is a message. I thought that I may have missed the Dane's promised phone call, but it is from my ex-husband. I've not heard the voice of this *first* Dane in over two years.

The message is for my son, who lives with me and is asleep upstairs.

My ex-husband sounds angry and asks that his call be returned that morning. He says that he is at the farm. But the machine doesn't shut off. It continues.

A phone rings and I hear my ex-husband say, "Hello? Hi Justine, how are you?"

"Fine."

"Well, I'll tell *you* something. You're fucked. Big time."

And he hangs up.

I press "9" *to save* and "end."

I panic, big time. I sit on my red bed and look at the white blinds.

I recall my message machine.

This second time, I hear a phone ring and my ex-husband saying, "Hello?"

Space
 "Hi Justine. How are you?"
Space
 "Well I'll tell you something. You're fucked. Big time."
 My answers aren't there!

I am confused as to what has just happened. After the message to my son, a phone had rung as if I had made the call. It seemed that my ex husband had answered the call, that he had addressed me and that I had answered. But my responses hadn't been recorded. He had set me up. I responded to a message he had left me. He had purposefully left adequate time between his assertions for me to reply. I hadn't been speaking to him at all. He had *meant* to scare me.

I wonder what has happened in his life to cause this outbreak, this flare.

It is 7 AM. I go downstairs to lock the doors and find my pepper spray. I see a note on the counter from my son who is still asleep. I read, "Mom, could you please leave me the rest of my allowance before you go to the gallery. I am going out to the farm to spend the night."

I imagine the ensuing night in the house, by myself, and I panic again. I want to call my Dane but I am afraid I will wake the family he lives with. I pray he will call me, but he doesn't.

I grip the pepper spray. My eyes narrow. My mouth sets firmly.

 My heart is beating like a rabbit's. I can see the dog coming.

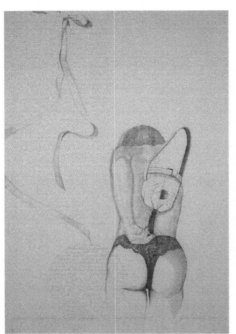

Chapter Fourteen
The Palms of His Hands

I begin by soaking the Dane's feet in an aromatic soapy bath. I have him bring his knees over the white enamel side of the tub and lay them on my white satin slip as I work on them.

I massage his soles and toes with an oatmeal peppermint scrub. I rinse away the grit with a wineglass of warm clear water. I cut his hard crusted toenails, those that I am able to press my way through with my inadequate clippers. I cover his shins and feet with a mint cooling gel. I burn, with the cool gel, the wound from the chain saw suffered that afternoon. He tells me this in retrospect as we lie on my bed.

He comes way too late. I come way too early.

I've been all around. I've been to Paradise and out the other side with no one to guide me, torn apart by the fire wheel inside me. But I won't hurt you, I won't hurt you.

The palms of the Dane's hands are a string of similes.

They erupt like volcanoes and form craters like the moon's surface. The white soaked skin flakes off like tattered lace in a coffin or a hanging macramé that has been left too long in the weather. Like rabbit skin glue after three days or bread in the summer, his palms are disintegrating in patterns like a damp elevation map. The white epidermis is like fish scales to be scraped off with a blade or soggy filo pastry. They are crumbling like a truck's muffler that has fallen off in the fall and is found again in the spring or like the bark on the stumps by the stream after the spring run-off. The top layer of skin can be peeled like the white fronds of a mandarin orange between the outer peel and the segments.

His palms are like nightmares bending over to strangle.

The skin is disappearing and joining the earth like the leather on the work gloves he'd left outside of his trailer, walked over by work boots and mouse paws and spider legs.

The palms of the Dane are a testimony to the timber frame that he is building. There should be a photo of his palms on the promotion poster. Pilgrims should place bouquets of wildflowers, light candles and pray for forgiveness.

The fact that he comes later, alone in his trailer, when I had come earlier and lost my grip - is not what impresses me. I am impressed by the awareness that this evening I never felt his palms touching me. There was no border between his skin and mine. There was no skin left, only fatigue from too much work.

It made no difference that I had pampered his feet. He was too tired. He needed his hands held.

This morning as I jog, I glare at a cat and still him from sketching into the headlights of the oncoming truck

Chapter Fifteen
A Pugnacious
Interjection

I am restless, waiting for a call from the Dane.
I could take on a lot tonight. I could ask the man in the Porsche to go for a drink. If I do, I will see him naked before the end of the night and he will have his way with me, whichever way he wants.

I have a filthy taste in my mouth, a nasty sensation from my sex. I could take on a motorcycle gang. They can spurt, spray, probe and penetrate me, I will laugh and wriggle like a maniac. I am feeling more than horny. I feel wicked and edgy.

The Dane is inaccessible. I have put in a call and he hasn't returned it. I want to ask him to go for a drink, not a cloying or supercilious invitation; I aim to devour his goodness or punish his badness. I will spin his head backwards and blast through the frozen half of his face. I will not only hurt him; I will torture him into succulent submission. He will acknowledge his match. We will shake hands firmly before I knee him in the groin and he knees me in retaliation. We will roll away from each other in agony.

I float above my anger for it has no ground in reason. It is seated in evasion. I want to strangle that which taunts me from a discernible distance and then scurries away. I need to pounce on a predator who won't deign to attack, being too busy mewing and slithering.

I wonder if the Dane is holding back, fearing I may become dependant. He has no cause to worry. Today, I am the spider, not the fly.

Chapter Sixteen
Dante
Making the Call /
Taking the Telephone

I wake up unsettled, restless and twitching.

I call Tiziano's office in Boston and am denied the pleasure of his voice with his chirpy secretary's salutation.

I call the Mongolian and am titillated by his loaded accent telling me to leave a message. He is not in the studio.

I call Dante in New York City. He answers defensively until I announce my name and his voice brightens. His shine lights me up. We exchange small talk.

He preloads his next question with "May I ask you something?"

"Of course, anything."

"What do you have on right now? Describe it to me."

I am striding around the back yard in the bright sunshine with the traffic heading for work on the far side of the fence.

"I have on my leopard print silk slip."

The truck drivers in high cabs can flash on my visual offering. They lift their hand from the gearshift and stroke their crotch.

"I've just come from the shower," he says. "I am sitting naked on a towel and I've grown hard as we've talked."

I walk through the kitchen and turn off the steaming kettle. I go up to my red room.

"Is your hand under your slip?"

"On the lips of my sex. My fingers are sliding on the soft slippery folds."

He turns me over with his words. He counterbalances my left leg. He accepts my back bending with a grand romantic gesture. He rushes my arrival by counting the strokes of his steps. His ballet shoes swish on the floor as he moves the length of his leg frontward and backward. I leap and he catches me. Keeping his balance he continues to twirl me into oblivion. When I slow enough to regain my focus, he pliés and rises with his thigh muscles distended. He groans, long and low, and collapses.

Silence crackles through the telephone hand set.

"I'll have to clean myself up. Once again, you surprise me, Justine. When do you return to New York?"

"In September."

"Ring me. I will return your call when I hear that you have arrived."

"You know, Dante, that there is no commitment in this fable. But, yes, I will call you in September."

Chapter Seventeen
The Dane
Insufficient Knowledge
and I Dream

The discordance between knowledge and being is my subject. There isn't any discordance in what directs the game. We are still caught up in the insufficiency of knowledge. It is what directs the game of encore – not that by knowing more about it, it would direct us better; but perhaps there would be better jouissance, agreement between jouissance and its end.

I have not seen The Dane in days, or heard from him. I know that he is occupied at the golf course where the tournament will pass by the site of the timber frame and the world will be watching him. I suffer, nonetheless, from *insufficient knowledge*. It is at the root of my restlessness.

Directly, The Dane has given me no signals of an impending ending other than warning me not to fall in love. This is my stated intent to him, as well, for our journey is to be one of *jouissance*. He has assured me that the need to remain secret in our affair is due to the recent birth of his daughter and the pining he endures on her account.

I am a public figure. To be known as "Justine Quercia's boyfriend" would be a spotlight on his being that he cannot at this point endure. I have been his solace. He values our relationship hoping that it will continue. But when he hears himself identified as "Quercia's" he is, in his word, "dis-attracted." This is the knowledge I am reacting to. It is insufficient and causes me anxiety.

His buoyant "Quercia, Quercia!" harkens his arrival. We fly into each other's arms and all of my doubt and restlessness dissolve in the immediacy of his physical frame. Only *jouissance* remains. I kneel and lay my lips on his navel.

As I rise from his belly button, he tells me of the undesired attention he has been receiving as the golf tournament is played out around his building site.

The owner of the golf course told him, "You don't need to wear a shirt, Dane. It is, understandably, too hot, this summer." His chest would, therefore, be on display, reeking of virility. The contrast of his packed mounds of muscle to the slack cloth of the golf shirts will have an impact. It is a marketing ploy.

He resents the attention. He declares he will shelter his heart under a shirt, cover his head with a bandana and wear sunglasses to obscure the blue beauty of his Danish eyes. He will have a manicure and not heft heavy logs. The lure of his ambitious charisma, his ardor to build, single handedly, the impressive timber frame is being tarnished by the aggressive promotion of a golf match. The studly aspects of his trade, stoked by his Viking personality will *not* be used to garnish a sideshow like a hooker in underwear declares the Dane. He declares he will smoke weed so he is stoned as the slack shouldered golfers follow the pros around the course past the work site. The resinous ash will outweigh the fresh air.

We have an agreement, the Dane and I. His calling "Quercia!" permits me to kiss his navel. The mounds of his chest are for my eyes only to rest upon. I notice the sun blisters and the dirt stuck to the sweat. His need to remain private, to order the feelings for his baby, is his testimony to me. He grants me trust with the immediate message of his willing body. The agreement between *jouissance* and its end is now based on sufficient knowledge.

We don't have sex for he must return to the building site with a load of materials.

At home, I am relaxed enough to nap, waiting for The Dane's promised, late night visit.

I dream that The Dane and I are on a front porch. My family and friends are gathered around. The Dane wraps his arm around my shoulder and turns me away from the gathering in a personal intimate gesture. He wants to kiss me. From the comforting, muffling, midnight blue of his sweater and the warmth of his chest, I am distracted by a danger call.

My ex-husband is there on the porch with us and when the Dane kisses me, my "ex" leaves the brightly colored setting. He steals my Harley and rides off on it. He determines a collision course with a thick cement wall. Family and friends gasp and I squawk "stop!"

He smashes, head on. Metal and his body collide with inert, gritty, hard matter. The dust clears to utter stillness and we see the Harley twitching like a man shot by a machine gun while my ex-husband walks off unscathed and with disdain as if disgusted by the kiss that he witnessed on the porch. The Harley shivers and dies.

I awake to a dusky quiet, understanding the meaning of the dream. I smile smugly at my knowledge.

I fall back asleep to the dregs of dreams. In this dream, I am arguing a good case in court against The Dane's independence. I condemn him to youth and a poorly constructed defense. But the court sides with The Dane. I loose and as I climb the stairs to yet another new apartment, I bemoan the loss of his chest on which to lay my head.

This discordant seepage is the limit to love and knowledge; it is the disagreement between *jouissance* and its end. It is the blind prophet ignoring the warmth of a helping hand and continuing to tap the tip of a cane on hard pavement.

Chapter Eighteen
The Dane
Squelching on the Heart

At the end of my bathtub there is an object of art, a chair.

It is a kitchen chair from the sixties with chrome legs and a padded seat and backrest. Originally, it was probably covered with a slick yellow or cranberry vinyl. The artist had removed this outer covering to reveal the beige flecked padding of the seat and back. On the felt padding of the seat, she sewed a white cotton heart. The stitches are clumsy. The thread appears to be soiled. From the bottom of the heart there is a curled shape of hair, like an inverted question mark. It seems to be a lock of brunette hair, a nice wave, but a closer inspection reveals that the form is made of a lot of curly pubic hairs clustered together. The seat was recovered in a clear vinyl so that the heart image with the curl would show through.

The Dane's asshole is squelching on the heart. His body is damp and warm, partly from the bath he's just gotten out of and partly from the muggy late evening heat. I am straddling his cock, which has been difficult to mount because of the downward hook it assumes when fully erect. But it is in me and I am bobbing up and down like a wild bunny, his strong arms helping to raise and lower my body. He is the color of slightly bleached mahogany. I am lighter, bronze as the Coppertone ad. I watch the hem of my lime green slip bounce up and down beneath which his strong male thighs, and my strong female thighs, frame the action.

His cock is warm from the bath, hot from his need, bigger, fatter and more forceful than I'd remembered. We haven't had sex in six days.

He bangs me on the doorframes as he carries me, still corking my sex, through two doorways and over the hardwood floors to my red bed. Then we copulate with no purpose other than sheer delightful sensation. There is nothing before and nothing after except the cum to lick off of his belly burnt brown from the midday sun of the golf tournament.

Chapter Nineteen
The Dane
Staking Territory

My black stocking describes a high arc as I swing my leg over the back of his motorbike and mount the seat. I press my crotch, exposed by the mini skirt, onto his ass and hold on around his superior stomach muscles, the result of six hundred sit-ups each day. The golf resort strains their eyes from behind discretely drawn curtains to watch as he drives me up the hill. We view the log cabin as we rise to the spot where I have parked my Harley to walk down to the work site.

The blonde cabin is, by now, eight feet high. The last round tops the window openings. The ridgepole, cooked crooked by the sun, lifts the thirty-foot logs up to the height. Adzed by the Dane, they gleam in the low cast evening light. He has one more round to adze and raise. He has one more week baking under the hot desert sun before he is to return to Denmark.

We glide along the golf paths, The Dane in his shorts, bronze feet in broken sandals, a light Danish leather jacket with no helmet, just a hat turned backwards, and me in my gold leafed Harley beanie, black jacket fringes flapping. We race the golf carts to the right-of-ways.

As we make the sharp turn at the top of the course he gestures to stop. From my noble mount, I respond, planting my feet on the ground to find there is no surface under the right boot. My beautiful orange Harley crashes to the ground. The metal weight smashes on the tarmac at the base of the "Show Home" sign with the bright green balloons. In the silence that follows when I turn off the key, he rips a balloon off and open. He sucks in the helium and sings *Love is in the Air.*

On this first ride with the Dane, he has to pick up my bike. He has to hold the hand brake while I turn the key to restart the engine. His helium song quacks out like a duck as he ties the shreds of the green balloon to my fender. It is a little tail flapping or a lizard tongue darting behind my hot ass as we ride into town.

At dinner, he is ruthless. He says I have told him three times that I don't trust him. He says that, just like a woman, I can't remember having told him this. He says I have prompted this outburst. I had asked why he trusted *me* and he said that he didn't, how did I like *that*? The first time I had told him I didn't trust him was when I'd confessed to anticipating a lump in my throat should he take another woman to dinner. So he says, as he sees it.

The immediate impact at dinner is of a hungry Dane chewing. He's used his body to earn his hunger. On the surface, right there before me, he consumes food into his body. His jaw is tense. I don't need to eat. I need to take off my jacket to show him my body.

His mystery is deep. His anger is evident. Still, I am his accomplice. We plot our crimes. I want a kidnapping, quite simply – the baby. He is hatching a plot to avenge his honor.

He's been smudged by Denmark's disinterested, somnambulist routines. As a young man he'd starved himself to become a fifty-one pound anorexic to prove a point. He remains invisible still to Denmark which maintains a moral decorum that denies the existence of his worldly soul. Denmark tightens the purse strings around possibilities and freedom. Denmark dares to defy this one curious Dane. He is bucking and testy as they prod him to closure. He refuses. Case is closed. His path hedges revenge. He is fearsome.

He must return to redefine Denmark. His Viking sword, forged in Denmark, has been tempered in new lands. It will flash as he swings it to illuminate evil. The fruit will not feel its skin fall away for his sword is sharpened with compassion. The flesh will only feel itself exposed and react to the cold.

In the comforting glow of my red room, The Dane admits that he trusts me, that he knows that I trust him. He admits to the anxiety that arises just before he leaves his adopted homeland, Canada, to return to Denmark. He takes me tenderly.

I, for sentimental reasons, keep samples of the Dane's cum sticking to my bedspread. I save the green shreds that fell off in my driveway to remind me of the quack of *Love is in the Air*. These momentos will help me in his absence for his sex is potent. It dissolves all desire like urine absolves the sting of the sea urchin. I lay in my bathtub and felt the warm golden liquid spread over my belly as he marked out his territory in this pioneer land.

Chapter Twenty
Post Partum

"Tonight is the end of the day that I woke up in the morning in the trailer of the Dane, after the last night spent with the carpenter rock star on tour" - it sounds like a sing song, a child's skipping game. But for me, it's a dirge.

Like a good *gopi,* I have stood beside The Dane as he created a legend in his own time. From the lush stage of the golf greens, he has strutted his stuff for the waitresses and chambermaids maintaining the expensive holiday homes that surround his worksite. He has choreographed his genius for the stunned onlookers.

Northern rock style, the rectangular shades with the mustard rims rested on the haughty bridge of his nose. An array of hats donned the skinhead pate - a tawny kerchief with a Celtic design, an earthen tone herringbone cap turned backwards, a brown felt bowler squashed flat.

The girls sent him notes with curls of their pubic hair. His potential for grandeur leaked through his radiant skin and foreheads bowed in awe of his brilliance. He shone like a pop idol protected within a shield of vibrations and remained inaccessible, flanked by the bodyguards of his difference. His far distant origins and his mother tongue guarded his right side. His untouchable integrity intimidated the superficial minions, repelling the adoration aimed at his left. His back was protected by the great wall of pain he had constructed in his solitude. It bounced the flames of idolatry back onto the fawners. The warmth was inviting but the barrier too hot to touch.

His chest was exposed. His straight-on stare met the onlookers with such clarity that the acidic blue brilliance blinded the feeble spectators and they lowered their lashes to fan his image. The striated blur gave a glimpse of the greatness of the Dane of carpenter fame.

He sits on the caramel rug of his trailer. His casual bronze legs below the blue boxers tap the beat of the tunes that define his perception.

He looks at me and smiles, "Quercia." I smile my sunshine back into the face of the Dane. I don't accept the pinhole perspective of a determined future, so I am able to look full in the face of the Dane. It is my privilege.

While the bug of "The Matrix" wiggles into the belly button of the actor on the screen of his television set, I lick my finger and twirl it in The Dane's navel. His limp hook grows big. The Pirate of Penzance takes my Canadian love song from all sides and coats my tummy with his opal splendor. I hold him from his back as he holds me to his back as we turn in the night on his narrow bed. I cup the muscled mounds of his chest through his sweater as he feels the fleshy mounds of my breasts through the sweatshirt he has given me to sleep in. I know him in the biblical sense. My hair has wiped the dust from his feet. The heater hums and warms our stocking feet as we breath in as much as we can hold our breath for, on the Dane's last night in the Canadian autumn.

The next day, Labor Day, the streets are silent. The alizarin apples lay on the viridian green grass. The peaches hang taut to the tree like the peach fuzz on the balls of the Dane.

Fanning the flames of fidelity has my sparks alighting in a disconnected burn. I spark on my destiny, my gender and my privileged perspective. I carry the phone with me in the early morning light hoping it will burst into flames and burn my palms with a soft Danish salutation. I flare up with the delivery man as he blushes from my heat.

I missed the Dane even before he left. By now he has passed through the airports, sat on the plane with his walkman tuned to the same channel as mine. He's gone back to Denmark, to his baby and the confrontation with the mother of his first born child.

Is his sword still sharp or does the bright garish sun of his homeland melt the firm resolve of steel? A soft baby's head can wilt the memory of a hand held in Canada.

I have weakened in the Dane's absence, fallen slightly ill. I am beset upon by petty particulars. I tried to bleach my teeth whiter and the gel seeped into my gums and left my jaw throbbing. I am in the company of couples and get drunk with the children. I sell my centerfold body to the aging community and observe the lascivious attention I receive from the merchants.

Dante calls from New York for telephone sex while my gallery is the venue for a television show on violence against women. The panting is broadcast to millions.

I have nothing to say. I have lost my voice.

I turn now to the songs that The Dane had taped for me and to the still photos of a blonde man frozen in front of the red walls of my bedroom. I reread the newspaper articles chronicling his accomplishments. I read my stories back to myself and am struck by my immersion.

I long to lay my hands on the chest of the Dane, to lay my head down and close my eyes.

Chapter Twenty One
The Dane
The Call that Was Not Made

The exterior front door light casts a beam through the window and illuminates the stairs to the second floor. The neighbor is out calling his cat and sees the red glow of my hair illuminated, a ghostly growing figure appearing past the front porch beam. My shoulders appear in the frame of the window and then my bare back as I climb to the second floor bathroom. My head disappears and the crack of my bum ascends the stairs. The whiter shade of pale of the back of my knees breaks the continuance from good thighs to nice calves. My back is sliced off from the top and the soles of my feet polka-dot the steps as they flip outwards towards the door. The show is complete and the man finds his cat.

My bath is warm and waiting and I slide into the comfort of the memories of the Dane.

I am surprised by his call for it has been only three days since he arrived in Denmark. I am surprised but expectant for the telephone is on the windowsill in the bathroom as I am lying in the tub and, because of its placement, I have been able to receive the call.

I tell him what he wants to hear. In his absence, I have learned nothing of his present state but inform him of his present absence. I have not had the voyeuristic pleasure of watching a man's nude body roll and flex in slippery bronze brilliance before my eyes, as he baths, not since his departure. I have not squatted and squirmed in the concave white enamel cradle as the golden shower of permissiveness glances off my thighs and shoulders, not since he left. Nor have I joked about a man's morning ablutions, not since his absence. His absence has been very present.

When he calls he tells me nothing informative. He adds nothing to the facts of his existence, only to the loss of his presence. I tell him of his absence. He tells me of his sense of lacking my presence. The Dane doesn't come through the telephone line; knowledge doesn't ring true, only the disembodied presence makes me aware of his absence, thrilling but unsubstantial.

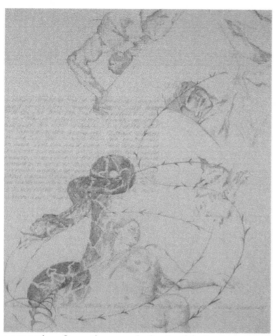

Chapter Twenty Two
The Punch of the
Proud Beaming Blonde

The blacksmith brings me a sheaf of photographs documenting the construction of the log cabin so that I can copy a few of The Dane in his absence. Within the stack of images of the Dane looking as I remember him and The Dane looking unrecognizable, is a photo of him in front of the Willies truck. The Dane is posed with his arm proprietarily placed on the shoulder of a proud beaming blonde. This beautiful young woman, I read as the mother of his baby, his nemesis during our summer love affair. The birth of the infant had coincided with the separation from the nonchalant pride he had exhibited as he rested his arm on her shoulder for the photographer to record "the perfect couple." As I pursue a talisman, a visual image to remember The Dane by, I unearth a voodoo doll.

The Dane is not present. My Viking has walked out. His photographs are drying on lines strung up in a dark room. Above my red bed the web has become a tangle of flapping photographs pegged to the sticky net. The mess of black and white photos caught in the gossamer thread obliterates the ceiling. The drizzle from the photographs have left the hardwood floors slippery and I miss my footing as I wander the empty house. I am lost in the tangle of cloying moments, my best-feet-forward are tripping. My progress is barred. I wander through indecent perfumes and downy chins and balls.

As I sheaf through the photographs, I can't cast my line out into this twisting crowd of magic minutes. The punch of the proud beaming blonde connects and renders me useless.

I leave my red room of hot memories and go to the bar where I dance myself into a frenzy, a froth of release. My tentacles perk up sensing the jazz guitarist lifting his leg with the minor chords like a kid having to pee. He comes over to talk as I draw in the line, hand over hand. Lassoed at the groin, he asks me for dinner.

Chapter Twenty Three
The Dane
Mulling Sex

My aim is to live in the present in order to receive knowledge of the present, untainted by a future expectation, or, an unsubstantiated interpretation of the present based on the past.

I can compare this aim to a color theory. As I acquire a past, a collection of experiences, a color is added to the present. The color could enhance the present and tint it or, if it is an opposite rather than an analogous color, it could taint the picture of the present.

The present, as a springboard to jump-start the future, can create a foundation for the future experience or, at the worst, obliterate the future experience.

Since my research is in the field of sex, my theory is applied to my research. Sex, felt through the physical and influenced by the mental, is potent in the experience (present), the memory (past) or the expectation (future).

My aim, to try and isolate these tenses, is conceptual only; for they exist, of course, as a continuum. Physically it is impossible to isolate them as the present series of NOW's. each contain a past and future.

Can I live in the present with the Dane without superimposing my translation of the past or my concerns for the future on that experience? My knowledge of the past can tint the present, render it fuller and more realized. The present, invested wisely, can tint the future. This task of color mixing acquires immense determination with no recipes or formulas available and the possibility of continuance as the sole aim of the exercise. This is the *encore* of woman.

Writing about sex, mulling it over, I feel the soft lips of my sex opening and closing, itching to be penetrated.

This is where *I*, Justine Quercia, have arrived at, as The Dane arrives back in Canada.

The Dane has returned! He steps out of my shower and stands in front of the vine mirror drying himself. As he holds the royal blue towel over his penis, drying his stomach muscles, his ass flexes in the reflection and his back ripples wet.

He flicks the indigo towel at my stocking-ed leg while his penis darts out from behind it's cozy covering. We don't have sex right away.

We continue on to an Italian restaurant, sitting at a table-for-two beside the old brick wall. The Dane begins by explaining the layout of the iron hooks that he would have the blacksmith imbed in the restaurant wall for him, if it was his place. The Dane would then tie me to them like Leonardo da Vinci's drawing, arms wide and legs spread. I would be naked. The Dane would sit on a chair in front of me, fully clothed. Periodically he would walk over and play with my sex, lick me and put his fingers up me. As I became excited he would walk away, leave me to cool down, and then return to sit on his chair and watch me, slowly undressing himself. Over and over again, he would stimulate me. When he himself had finished undressing, he would punctuate his titillation of my genitals by playing with himself. He would stroke his penis slowly and provocatively until he was about to come, then stop, rise, and visit me again, licking and fluttering his fingers in the folds of my vagina. I would be at the shore of release and he would back off in the light of my trembling desire. Again he would sit and masturbate.

" Do it to me! You must. Let's go home, I can't stand this." I am unable to swallow the salmon pink, creamy fettuccini while he tells me the story.

"I'm greasing the gears for later, Quercia. Eat slowly. Chew your food and savor it, as I am now savoring the expectation of you, Justine Quercia, after this long separation. For now, just listen, for I am greasing the gears for later."

He says he would like playmates. We discuss the option of his biker friend having sex with me at the same time. I offer to do so.

"The lamp black hair of your brawny biker friend would brush my spine as he took me from behind while I rode you, your golden blonde balls pounding my henna red pubic hair flat. You could blindfold me but I would know who was where by the furry feel of your pelts…"

We mull the potential of my sister, Juliette, joining us, with her new boyfriend, a musketeer. His chestnut ponytail and moustache would compliment the peachy lips of my sex with the Danes lance in my mouth. My sister's ass, pierced by the rapier of her gallant musketeer would be softened by the darting parries of the Dane's lilting tongue. The bleached maple blonde of his goatee would grow stiff as her juices dried after we had fallen apart from our puzzled formation.

"Yes, and I will take on the waitress, tumble her bones!" The wine is finished. "Please, waitress, the bill!"

While the Dane goes to pay the bill, I look frankly at the handsome businessman as I rise from my chair. I lock his gaze as I draw the hem of my black mini skirt down over the tanned skin at the top of the lacey stockings. I see his lashes flicker as he glimpses the Venetian red satin of my panties.

The Dane asks for a chair as we enter my red bedroom. I bring in the one from the bathroom, the one with the curl of pubic hair pressed under the vinyl.

We perform every act we had choreographed earlier in the restaurant. The cum ricochets off of the red walls and soaks the red sheets. His, floods my bed and the mattress grows heavy: mine, geysers and steam-cleans his pistons and muscles.

We have stopped talking. We are left staring at the dripping walls, running with passionate emissions. We breathe and we sigh and we mop the sweat from our foreheads. We sigh and roll over away from each other.

Not a thought is spoken. We have drained our lust.

Chapter Twenty Four
Dante
Between Rehearsals

I return to New York to set up my newly acquired, sight unseen apartment.

"He died in the back of a taxicab," says Lucio, describing the previous tenant as I drink wine and eat prosciutto and melon in his establishment.

The Sicilian restaurant downstairs from my newly rented apartment had hosted the previous tenant nightly for dinner and often for lunch as well. Lucio, the third generation owner of *Pozzi Ristorante,* had greeted this tenant, cheek to cheek, clasped hand over handshake as he entered, stepping onto the square inch black ceramic tiles with his good Italian shoes.

Now, Raphael, the super for the building, is at the top of the ladder fixing the light I had inadvertently pulled from its housing while trying to mount a decorative umbrella. He, too, tells me that the previous tenant died in the back of a taxi. That tenant's mother had died in my apartment, the apartment with the sparkly wiring presently absorbing Raphael's attention but, not to be spooked, the latest tenant had died in the back of a cab.

"Yeah, he didn't go out much. He was diabetic, always ate downstairs. He was one of dose guys, know what I mean?"

"One of those guys? No. What do you mean?"

"One of *dose guys*! They bumped him off in the back of a taxicab. You know - the mob."

It's hard to find an apartment in New York, especially in the Village. They rarely come free without a tenant already lined up to move in. Unless somebody dies. The mob had done me a service. I would consider it a privilege to live in this miniscule space. I would continue my research into the limits of love and knowledge with a diligence worthy of the apartment's colorful history. In between appointments I would explore the loose floorboards for treasures left in an untimely fashion by the previous tenant.

It takes five New York days to set up the apartment, finding sweet smelling pillows, setting roach and rat poison and scrubbing the tiny tiles on the bathroom floor. Despite his eager invitations, I have no time to meet with Dante between rehearsals.

I return to Canada.

Dante calls Canada to say he regrets having not seen me in New York. We undress over the telephone. He is in shorts and a T-shirt, lying on the floor of his eighty-ninth street apartment with New York pitch black and still steamy hot outside the open window. I watch the dusk grow to darkness through the window panes in my red room in Canada, which becomes littered with my dove gray jeans, skinny T-shirt, lime lacey bra and g-string. My high heels clunked onto the hardwood floor. I am wet from the moment my finger touches myself. He has been hard since he began dialing.

Later, I leave the warm damp impression of the cheeks of my ass on my red sheets, smiling as I rise to dress. The cum soaks my panties and the crotch of my pants as I don my high heels. I walk through the grocery store pushing my cart and smelling my sex as my intimate lips squelch when they meet and separate and meet again. The perfume of Dante's arousal is left by the cornflakes and creamed corn in the Canadian evening.

Book Three
Editing Evil

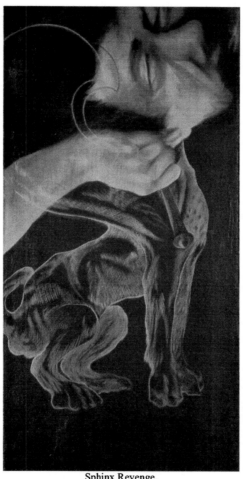

Sphinx Revenge,
oil on canvas, 36"x 18"

Editing Evil

This devotional documentation requires a human sacrifice. Just as God called Abraham twice, "Abraham, Abraham," and demanded from him the life of his only son - and just as Abraham, never questioned his worthiness for the sacrifice would prove his devotion to God - so my research continues.

The human sacrifice is obvious. I am granting to this quest the gift of my experience. I, Justine Quercia, am sacrificing my life, my time.

I am featuring and sharing my blood. The careful journal entries, the immersion in sexual permissiveness and risk-taking, the willingness to perhaps become a loathed being, an unwomanly, immodest woman; has a grand and arrogant precept.

I am presuming that I am the one called upon to offer a sacrifice. I have shaped my circumstance and physicality to this end. I have been granted the opportunities to pursue my path of knowledge. I am operating with blind faith that it is I who will perform, that the casting director has chosen me from those who had auditioned. Now I am writing the script as I speak the lines.

The narrative is an epic. This is an important piece of literature. It deals with the beautiful and the sublime and it is within the nature of the sublime to be beyond comprehension.

My choices are able to be more extreme as I am offered a wider range of possibilities to further my research into the limits of love and knowledge.

Even if I were to find an editor for this material, I doubt that it would clarify the results of this research

Chapter One
Editing Precedents

The Dane

The Dane, a respite from promiscuity, has informed me that we cannot continue.

"I am not sufficiently Italian to sport you as my Canadian mistress while I receive my wife and our baby daughter into my frontier home." He weeps and tears the golden hair from his magnificent chest, but it makes no difference. He must assume a distance from me and cleanse his palette so that he is able to discern if the taste of his future is tart or sweet.

I must learn to survive without him in my life, until he comes knocking at my door.

So, I must continue.

I am obsessed with my fearful research. There is no shame, no sense of immorality. My fear is a mortal fear, a fear of being completely sacrificed by the ardor of my curiosity. I have already laid love on the sacrificial altar.

I am coming forward to be transfigured. It is time for a metamorphosis created by my need to change the very definition of love and sexuality.

I want to continue.

I don't want to be sacrificed. I want to live a brand new life. I don't want to die.

My Editor

My Editor was, at first, a stranger to me.

He came into my gallery having seen March in the *City Calendar* where I am mounted on my Harley in a g-string, sunglasses and gloves. During our first week, he

edited "Gentle Bondage" and "Lay My Head on the Chest of the Dane." He edited
my secret erotic confidences before I have even seen him naked. Yet I anticipated his
arousal as he read and so he became My Editor.

He tells me that he has, in his own way, sucked off men for money, that he is
conversant with eroticism.

His profile is haughty. His gait is pumped. His arms, when he removes his
jacket are naked male biceps appearing intrusive from the ragged cut sleeve of a
white cotton shirt – a surprising anecdote to the tailored blazer, the urbane style that
first entered my gallery. His eyes are sloe eyes, almond open and cockeyed
confidant.

There's something about him that feels shady. In another ten years he may be
the scoop of the dogged reporter who makes his million off the story of the discovery
of a dead heiress.

But My Editor swears he won't be the death of me.

Nonetheless, he typifies the confidence of a con man. He bites the flesh from
my lips as he kisses and pouts his way into my heart. He plans my mutilation. He
asks me over to his cottage on the lake for dinner. He delivers the assignation in a
bouquet of flowers set in sprung cedar boughs - snapdragons, tiger lilies, baby mums
died puce and fuscia. They are as sweet as frangipani in front of a police station in
the tyrannical dictatorships of the third world. They smell as sweet as the danger of
tomorrow when I will drive in a sports car to the outskirts of the city, the end of the
beach. I am planning to have sex for the first time with a man whose words have
taunted my discretion and cancelled all fidelity to honest liaisons.

On our first date, after a wonderful dinner that he has cooked, we take an after
dinner stroll. We come together on the end of his dock, the lake shining with the
reflection of the full moon above. A typical scenario, we kiss long and lusciously as
my hands wander inside his coat and his inside mine.

My habit has been to eat what is put before me and yet as I move forward to
swallow my desire he counters my step with "I should walk you to your car."

I yearn, groan inwardly and tilt my ass up in invitation as he hands me into my
sports car. I want to know him *now*. But he assumes an editorial position and
stultifies my prose. He inserts the first of many commas. He predicts a better blaze,
flicks his seemingly coquettish fan above my smoldering and I have no recourse but
to back out of his driveway. I contemplate the denial of his illuminated courtyard as
the big wooden gate swings closed.

A few days later, I have My Editor secured between my red sheets. I can conduct an exploration, an anatomical analysis. I can study the tattoo draped across his shoulder, a sample of Japanese erotica on relatively white skin while he spends a silent night. I acquire a subtle attachment to his body, to the particular way his flesh fills up to the top of his skin, to his curves and embraces. I decide that he is worthy of a journey past his arrogant exterior. I may find in him, a sexual sage. It is my destiny.

An editor should know how to eliminate the inessential, to eradicate obfuscation. An editor should pare down the superfluous and uncover the essence of articulation. This editor, My Editor, does this between my red sheets. Although I resent his cuts and slashes, I am impressed by his censorial powers. He holds me at bay until I have exuded such a potent emanation that I am in danger of divulging the ending, out of context. I suck on his stem; it grows osmotic and throbs towards the tip, the potential budding joy of springtime. Then just as I am open mouthed to receive his virile excretions he disengages my mission and brings my mouth to his full sensual lips. He kisses me into oblivion and then he leaves my tongue searching the air for his flesh as he begins his voyage down my supine body. He drills my nipples, performs a root canal with nitrous oxide and brings me to a giddy pain. A full-throated head-back melody echoes from my rosy tunnel and I overflow onto his face.

Mercilessly, he reviews this paragraph again and again. Just as I feel deserving of his viscous blessing, he pulls me away from the host. He slashes, with his cruel pen, yet another extremely important word to which I am pitifully attached. "Explode," "projectile," "spurts" and splashes" or phrases to which I am longing to succumb - "all over me," "bursts forth," or "to which I inevitably echo" - all fall on the cutting room floor. He stills my overeager vocabulary and leaves on my pages a single ripe fruit, which is sure to spray seeds from its juicy readiness when it finally falls. My editor transposes my tense to the future anterior while he craftily loads his dice.

I experience superlatives and mix metaphors.

The Dane

A change in place, a switch in character and The Dane reappears. The blonde has come and gone and they never touched each other except through the periphery of their child.

Up from the abyss of pathos, he stands shining in his Viking health and Nordic splendor. He has slain his dragons and recaptured his legend. The tangled rat's tails disengaged as the babies chewed their way free of their siblings. His helmet is polished and reflects the new land, the Canadian frontier. He springs forth rejuvenated as if he has not lost a day of sleep pining and mulling over the fate of his family.

I fall into his arms. I clasp the mounds of his chest in the cultivated palms of my hands and we weep at our wounds, suffered in mutual absence. He is worthy of worship. He is in from the dessert. He has never betrayed me. He has drunk only water from the golden goblet that I gave to him on the day he declared he could see me no more. He has eaten cacti and lizards.

And true to his promise, he is as hard as an ox, as lustful as a pirate who has been six months at sea. He mounts me like a tiger. He is as long as an elephant. His arms hold my weight as he raises and lowers me, dipping into my vessel and slipping out to fresh air, over and over. He pounds rhythmically. He is in forward and backward. He attempts the fifty-four positions from the Kama Sutra and accomplishes fifty-two, rolling two into one. He is loaded with sperm. He is bursting his seams. He reclaims his booty with finesse and no questions.

I've been away. He's been away. Now we're back home, screaming and moaning, grunting and grinding our way to release.

Chapter Two
His Legendary Tail

My Editor

I am a cultural snob. I pass the lower, coarse, vulgar, venal, sensual experience through the disinterested filter of taste. I have acquired money and social position, which allows me the time and the privilege of scribing my impressions. I am an artist and taste is a determinant front-liner. I am sufficiently detached from a struggle for survival to assume an avant-garde stance.

I have a natural disposition towards belief. I willingly immerse in experience to the point of near oblivion, knowing that I am able to extract myself before I loose my sense of identity.

I am a consort for Titans, surreal manifestations of extreme personality and character. I have sex with aristocrats who are unattached to heritage through arrogant dissimulation. They grant me the objective view necessary to maintain my documentation of consortiums.

My editor embodies this Titanic ethos. Just as an actor can derive the ultimate impact from the use of a throwaway line, so his physicality is relaxed and not inhibited by stage directions. His taste exists in relation to his class and always reflects his aristocracy. Whether he is in black jeans, a cut off shirt and bare feet, an ethnic vest and hand tailored shirt (one of twenty hanging, pressed and ready) or an Armani suit, he breathes with the same unconscious wheeze. He cannot lower his chin.

His carnal knowledge is extensive. His quest to explore is an Aristotelian gift bestowed upon a promising student. He is able to wear his depravity on his sleeve. His nobility sanctions it.

A hotel clerk is swiping over my visa card at the desk of the Grand Hotel. An element of compromise hangs over the transaction and politicizes the payment. This hotel is luxurious and the veneer is an expensive sheath on a grandiose architecture. We have been to the Symphony Ball. My glossy-lipped glamour with plucked eyebrows and crimped red hair, hangs on the arm of his tuxedo. The pimply clerk gains bezazz as My Editor banters. The star struck fan hands him back the warm card and the key.

I am the lady to his gentleman. He is the Tennessee walker, looking down from the bridge of his nose to the outline of our evening. Tonight, for the first time, he has brought out a paper packet from his cigarette pack. He scoops with the nail of his baby finger and I lean over to snort the forgotten substance. With the white dusty chalk, we map a trail. I recognize the familiar lump at the back of my throat, a nasal drip of self confidence.

Now, lines later, we make a grand entrance to the applause of bed linen in a neutral hotel room. We pick up the trace left by the moon on the dock and the seemingly endless repetitions of my, one-sided, coming.

His legendary tail exudes from the base of his very smart spine at the southerly tip of his medulla oblongata. It coils back into his body after recesses. It returns to be educated in cunning and strategy. The next time it appears there is a novel plethora of cutting and scathing adjectives.

The curl of his lip responds to the curl of his tail. The upper lip rises, not deigning to show teeth and his nose tilts upwards. This seductive sneer matches the calculating approval that lurks under his eyelids. There is an absence of focus to his gaze. The object, and indeed it is an object rather than a subject, is blurred as he tunes into his personal agenda and listens for messages from his sensual spirit guide.

He is complete and unadulterated in the moment. He is, after all, the sovereign head. His attention is besought by minions who cannot resist the temptation of a dance with the devil. He is the purveyor of the wit and brilliance of God. He is granting a visit, drawn to the common realms of desire where he manipulates the push and pull, the attraction and disgust of humanity. He has a fine calf tattooed with a dark band designating rank. He approaches the bed with the casual pomposity of a brat.

The Tantric seduction of his fleshy corporeal presence transmits a message of permissiveness and indulgence. Touch is a languish. Pressure is perfected. Pain is precise. I submit. I succumb. I faint and revive to open the door to the shining foyer of his celestial home. The suffused grace of his hospitality impresses my impoverished vision. Exploration is infinitely possible.

My nipples protrude as the cool air wafts from the lifelines crossing his palms. They snap to attention and assert their dominion. They pop like a cork over full-bodied wine, rich drinking, ripe tasting, delicious.

I have always been secure in my sexual pacing. I have sensed the appropriate manner to stroke and lick, to encourage a man to release. I have been with men whose coming marked the success of my technique. All of my stories have been 'cum tales.' They have ended in climax. There can be a successive occasion to build towards a new peak, but still they have ended with ejaculation.

This time it is different, for although I have felt the first drops of premature sperm pulsing from the generous tip of My Editor's penis, I have not yet been covered in, swallowed or internally received his cum. He has not ejaculated. I am still challenged.

I run my tongue from the tip of his superb stem down the throbbing vein and lick his balls. I slither my kitten lapping back up again, circling the tip and dipping into the mewing orifice tasting the salty droplets. The rush of his sexuality is palpable beneath the velvet surface of my tongue. I receive messages from the ridge of virility, which I travel again and again. As he brims, my pelvis rocks in response. My sex is yearning and striving towards his magnificent organ. He builds in length, in breadth, in the dimensions of his desirability. I am yawning open, bending backwards for his omnipotent gesture. He achieves and succeeds and conquers and rules without contention. Then his hands pull my torso to his chest, my lips to his mouth and he enters me moving with a supernatural motion, awakening the earth with his volcanic potential. I grip his hard cock between my eager vaginal walls. He wanders my succulent hills and burrows into regions of perverse respect. I cinch my obsession to his driving sweet thrusts and squirt golden kisses in the face of his penis. The flurry of unending rushes and withering overwhelms me. I loose my memory. I forget who I am and clamor only for what is more and less. The pleasure riddles my body and I twitch and shiver as each nerve is punctured. He attains supremacy and secures my unending devotion. He repeats himself and commands me to sacrifice after sacrifice until I am reduced to a shameless seduced woman with the eminence of a visionary promoting a new religion. This drug is so intense it severs, completely, my ties to time, to place, to anything other than his particular sex.

And yet still, I have not been baptized. My knowledge of his satisfaction is unusual. The closure of ejaculation has not transpired. He leans towards me and it all begins again – the cyclical coming, going and coming.

My Editor has forced me to question what these anecdotes about sexual encounters have to do with a pursuit of knowledge? Indeed, is it not a philosophical pretense to transfer the significance of interpersonal physicality into the highest form of pure and unapplied thinking?

I assert my righteousness.

"We are discussing things seriously here and if you won't deign to give me your attention I will drop your acquaintance. I will retreat into my underground hole."

I may be impressed, but I have an upper hand as well as the one that is stroking him. I will bring him to his shuddering sensual knees. I can be patient, but I will know him eventually. It is part of my mandate: *I believe that during the life of an artist, a poet, a dancer there will be lovers. The lovers, too, will be poets or musicians, artists or actors. They will be great lovers because they are true musicians, poets, dancers and artists. The simpatico is so great that it reveals they are lovers. They don't have to stay or remain true or continue. They just have to come and their beauty is revealed.*

I have become very busy and must carry a calendar and make bookings for my sexual time.

The Dane

I dine with the Dane. I dress for him in my most alluring short tight skirt and a blouse that enhances my cleavage. He likes this, the high heels, the outfits, my slight femininity beside his muscular body. He takes pleasure in the contrast of my birdlike fragility to his mass. He senses the heads turning as we pass by and he preens. He likes to pick me up and carry me over thresholds.

He carries me throughout the evening; into my bedroom, from the bed to the chair and back to the red sheets. He moves me on the bed attached to his chest like a baby monkey, entwined. His musculature resonates. His body is brilliant, his skin oiled, the golden down glistening and filtering the light like sunshine behind bean sprouts. He pours himself completely. He gushes ardor. He indulges himself with a full, unadulterated take-over of my fragile frame. I yield to his embrace, to his mouth and his virile emanations. He releases as my milky secretion caresses his penis.

The Dane never stays over night. But tonight, his eyes close and his breathing becomes steady and sonorous. Having sex with the Dane is usual, to observe him asleep is a phenomenon and I am placed in an absurd position of responsibility. Would he like me to wake him?

The bed is more accustomed to My Editor. I feel I am cheating. Gently, I nudge.

The yellow lashes flutter open and the azure blue consciousness climbs out.

"Thank you, Baby. I have left my heater on. I must leave."

He rises. He dresses and for now, he leaves my red sheets. His goblet is in the back of my kitchen cupboard, safe until he decides to take it with him. No one else will use it, but for now, the red sheets will cover the warmth of another.

Chapter Three
Closing the Tantric
Circle

Dante

When he was young he had a small dog. Dante was continually horny, his cock swelling at the slightest provocation. He put his adolescent throbbing member between the hind legs of his small faithful companion and within seconds, he ejaculated. He felt sorry and there was no recourse for an apology to his trusting female canine. The memory humiliated him, haunted him, yet he could tell about it and I could appreciate the telling.

My Editor

Finally, his Tantric habit is detoured!
He ejaculates in my mouth, a hot gulp of semen.

Warm essence swelling my cheeks, overflowing dams of white enamel, tunnels down my esophagus and radiates heat from my navel. I inevitably echo. I insert my phrase with rich bountiful gusts. I marvel to receive this searing munificence.

And miraculously! - his body has not turned corpse cold. I have not drained him of his essential temperature with his virile flushed emanation. Such human warmth invaded the cavity of my mouth that I suspected I had surreptitiously stolen his life entirely. But still, he breathes.

I had twirled my tongue leisurely, slowly testing his response. I coolly calculated his moans and tempered my pace, licking slowly. I pampered his penis with care giving perception. I dwelt on the pressure required to pull up with my palm squelching on his male muscle. I kneaded my dough with the love of a baker infusing a wedding cake with a fertile future. I visually extended the sperm until a potential fetus imitated his energy. I coaxed his virility. I coddled his stem. I gave my undivided attention. I idolized his cock, its pure phenomenology with the inherent character of creation. I sunk into depravity. I transcended skin and body fluids. I discovered the roots of pagan idolatry. I visited the Far East and met consorts of kings. I minced as a geisha and serviced the emperor. A lip glossed cheerleader after the game, I went down on my knees before the athlete who scored all the baskets to the sound of applause from the bleachers.

This time, I am able to relate his ending to that which I know - he came.

He rolls over and sleeps.

I too, used to gush and descend immediately to the status of an untouchable. My editor taught me how to stretch the sensation, to hang onto every word of a long rambling river sentence.

Can I breach his authority, which I complicity ordained, and lead him down a primrose path of ejaculatory dalliance? Is there indeed such a phrase? He entered the game to play, to leap, bound and score. He dribbled with interminable generosity, causing me to come repeatedly, repeatedly. Now I've sunk a basket. Is this the final score or the start of a new tournament?

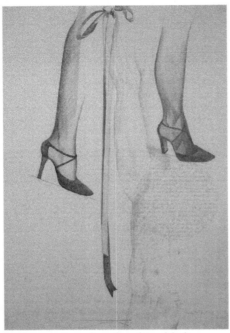

Chapter Four
A Thin Line of Fresh Blood

"Raccoon
The lovable scalawag is a favorite
of mine with its black mask, ringed tail
and sly cunning ways. Using many crisp,
dark and light strokes, I render the thick
bushy coat. The face is fox like with a
dark streak up the forehead. The coon is
nosy, daring and resourceful."

My Editor

My ex-husband is playing the drums in the Bistro and from the outside he is illuminated on the stage behind the plate glass window like a drugged whore in a peep show.

My Editor leads me in. I saw Little Richard led into a show by a handler in just this way - his black frizz had bobbed past me as he minced and avoided eye contact. I too, feel mincing and superficial.

My ex-husband registers that it is I, his ex-wife, being led towards him by this tall handsome young man, My Editor. My ex-husband freaks and escapes from our dandy-ism.

Despite my sense that this invasion of my ex-husband's territory has been superficial, I feel liberated. I have batted the severed head of the last cruel act of my ex-husband from the body of our marriage. My Editor has led me through the door of the Bistro and I plant a juicy kiss on the scalawag's masked visage. I can once again have a glass of wine with my friends.

My Editor's agenda has been quite different for the bistro is where we will meet our connection, Carlotta. He had to bat the head of the house out of the way before I would be able to score.

We have scored and snorted.

My black high heels are filling with new fallen snow as we cross the wind swept width of the city street between one club and the next. The sky is a lime gray illuminated by street lamps. The red signal light is stuck on all four directions.

I am having difficulty catching up to his predetermined stride with my hip gimped from a five o'clock fall over the open door of the dishwasher. My surface is indiscernible to the inside of my head, to conscious me. I am a shell reversed. I exist only as an interior. I am a raw impression of myself. As I enter the club and trail behind my date, The Editor, I dribble a thin line of fresh blood that alerts the wolves to my presence. Nostrils tilt back to receive a whiff of my passing. Eyes narrow in on potential easy prey, a wounded doe.

My Editor is burnished with a rough patina. His pulse is accelerated. He is entering the arena ready to wrestle the lions - for sport. I am leaning towards his protective shoulder proud of, yet confused by, the impact of his swagger. I can barely visualize a lion, much yet anticipate an encounter. I am awash on a muddy pool of vulnerability and the bar seems peopled with stupidity and lechery. I am not a good playmate and yet can't take my toys home because I have left them behind, somewhere or other.

My needs are simple although not sufficiently clear for articulation. Only in retrospect can I face this crisis. I struggle to remain polite to the drunken media man who is buying our drinks. I smile the phoniest of smiles at all of the approaches. Every time I advance forward I encounter another eager-to-engage devotee. I am an utter imposter, waving the queen's wave and greeting the blurry citizens of an alienated republic.

My Editor says he is going to dance. He doesn't ask if *I* would like to dance. He doesn't bend his head to mine and touch my fringe with his intelligent brow. I loose whatever vestige of tolerance for the workings of the world I had possessed, as I recoil into my introspective, womanly being.

I admit to defeat.

I mewl in response to his superior catcall. I skid on the snow, shaking and shivering from cold drafts. I cry in front of him. My voice rises and veers towards a screech. I panic and fly sideways with no control of my steering, right through the intersection.

My editor patiently picks up my pieces and plows through the rubble. He operates the Jaws of Life and pries me loose from my recently careening vehicle. My spine is snapped and I have lost all potential for achieving a dignified stature. But the revelation of the close call with annihilation is invigorating. I am granted a new opportunity to greet the unforgiving light of day without a cowl. I am not beholden. No prisoners were taken. I am weary and recovering.

Chapter Five
Catch the Smart, Tart

Dante

It is late at night as I return to New York and my message machine is full.
I focus on Dante's - "Call me, no matter what the time is."

I open the door and espy a disarmingly naked visage ascend from the stairwell. It is indeed Dante, my challenging guide, discovered last year in the church as The Priest cleansed my sins, and maintained over the telephone during my sojourns in Canada.

He prods and pokes at my life with a lewd curiosity. As he reads from *Gentle Bondage,* my first book where our erotic relationship is documented, he vacillates between wounded respect and an evident attempt to understand me. He takes every subject just a scary step or two beyond an acknowledged boundary. His questions concerning my sexual disposition veer on libel. He is seeking slander. He has incest on such a rapid boil, he comes close to ruining my stew. He turns up the element. But I, too, sense the potential to set off the smoke alarm and place my lighter back in my pocket, allowing him to strike his matches as he needs them.

The inevitable happens with a smell of sweet violence. He uses his fingers like he's banging his head against a wall. He snuggles them in my asshole seeking a depraved solace. He backs off only to draw the condom over his erection which he thrusts into my sex with a sigh of relief. His rhythm is an onslaught rather than a pleasure. He uses two condoms, for one rips in the grip of his anxious obsession.

I come first. There is no discipline in this session. Then he comes, gets up and cleans up thoroughly, wrapping the condoms back in their wrappers.

He asks if we can meet again before I leave New York. He has no interest in meeting my friends or family. He shudders at the aspect. Being an actor, it is a subtle shiver, causing the cloak that he shakes before my invitations, to shimmer.

I have never been to Dante's place. He always comes to me. The greatest trick the devil ever pulled was convincing the world that he doesn't exist. Dante exists only when he decides to visit. And he visits to have sex with me, Justine Quercia, a woman who is older than his mother.

As he leaves he declares repetitively that I am "a nice lady".

I wonder if Dante is losing direction? Am I still his 'Beatrice'?

Or, am I his nemesis? Am I a she-wolf, giving him a glimpse of flesh and then twirling to reveal a transmogrified harpy? Is he splitting in two and taking the first path as well as the second? And where does this leave *me* if he is my guide?

Dante telephones and disturbs me from a deep unconscious sleep at three in the morning. He asks what I am doing. Customarily, I am lost to the beckoning call of service seekers, conversations or solicitations at three in the morning. I tell him this and then answer his question as to my attire.

"I am, by habit, naked in my bed, just as you left me yesterday evening, lying on my belly with my thighs shivering from your release."

Dante speaks. "Jenny is with me. She is my lover and we are having sex. I want you as well, Justine. Make yourself wet. Play with us baby."

"Can I speak with her, Dante? I want to hear her voice. I want her to tell me what she is doing, where her mouth is, what her fingers are touching."

He calls her name as if she is down a hallway or in the kitchen.

A falsetto voice answers. "No. I don't want to speak with her."

The voice is disembodied and a parody of a woman's pitch. I know beyond a doubt who is talking. I believed him when he introduced himself as an actor.

We tango. I'm the foil. With resilient juiciness I squirm into my role and probe my crannies.

'Jenny' pants and moans in a rhythmic syncopation to Dante's deeper groans. Her drag-queen-bunny-cries fire round for his round. He groans guttural ecstasy and she counters with mimetic castrato warbles. As Dante comes in verbal spurts, she matches him cry for cry. Like a donkey braying, the voice is high then low, high to low, high, low.

Dante verbally guides me through it once more and we both come again. 'Jenny' is not vocal this time.

"Where was 'Jenny' that time?" I think. "Did Dante swallow her whole? Eat her all up?"

The next day, when I insinuate my suspicions as to Jenny's virtual reality, Dante hangs up on me.

I have to catch the smart, feel the sting. He had felt unsure to me from the outset, the penultimate one night stand that we had eked out through impersonal telephone encounters.

Dante's angry. Now I must truly feature my blood, shame, curse and humiliation. I have been denied a dignified closure on perversity. I am cast, like Lisa from Dostoevsky's *Notes from Underground*, as a prostitute, a tart, used by a young man with no scruples whose fear of the sublime induces him to severity. But unlike Dostoevsky's "Lisa", I am not the creation of an author. I *am* the author.

I walk to the *Guggenheim Museum* and twist my way through many years of gorgeous Armani gowns. I consider Dante.

When Dante relates his experience to me I doubt the veracity of his stories. More than this, I don't believe them. There is an element in the scenario that is too fantastic, yet I enter into the game and play along. I hope to glean some garnet of wisdom from this convoluted meander.

Conversely, as I relate my daily experiences to Dante, I can sense *his* disbelief. How ironic, for as I talk with him, I also am listening to the absurd caricature that I must represent to him. Yet my stories are indeed true and my life - fantastical.

At the base of the *Guggenheim* spiral, I dial Dante's number from the phone booth and when he answers, he says he is sorry.

My Editor

When My Editor relates his experiences to me I am teased again and tempted by doubt. How could these tales be true? They are rife with superlatives, suicides, bikers, brilliance, glib arrogance and the shattering and splintering of glass at dawn as his body lies prone in a cupful of blood on my bathroom floor

I am writing about My Editor anticipating that he will read and edit that which I have written. Knowing that he will read the transposition of our mutual experiences after it has passed through my strangely meshed filter, I temper my stories. I turn up the instruments that sound sweet and low to my ear and mute the discordance. I perform an original mix on My Editor.

My Editor is laced with lines, white cocaine reference points. Cross referencing the names, balancing the columns, placing the active physical editor belly to belly with his ethereal, elusive story line only serves to reinforce incredulity. He cannot be this awesome, freaky and beautiful and yet he appears to be so.

"His butter sticks to my spoon as I circle the bowl." I write.

"It picks up my sugar and the glass sides loose their covering. My eyes, level to the countertop, peer through the mixing bowl and my mouth salivates. The cake will be iced. Elaborate decorations in pale green, lemon yellow and robin egg blue will match candy stripe pink. This cake will rest in my stomach and issue waves of well being for, perhaps, fifteen minutes. The icing sugar numbs my tongue.

Then a ripple in the stasis disturbs clarity. Doubt encroaches on the holistic food value. Bloating creeps through consciousness and the realization that it was not such a good idea to have ingested this mixture dawns. Breathing is stifled, squashed by my obese stomach.

Gods eat angel food cake. Accustomed to bread and simple goat cheese, the injection of icing and feathers can be a traumatic culinary shock."

My Editor, when he edits this, will either throw up or sit back, satiated and satisfied.

The rumors are spreading about women who have sex with their editors.

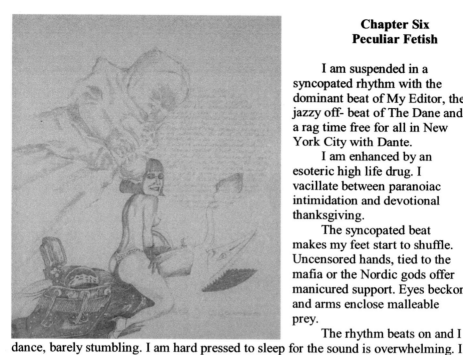

Chapter Six
Peculiar Fetish

I am suspended in a syncopated rhythm with the dominant beat of My Editor, the jazzy off- beat of The Dane and a rag time free for all in New York City with Dante.

I am enhanced by an esoteric high life drug. I vacillate between paranoiac intimidation and devotional thanksgiving.

The syncopated beat makes my feet start to shuffle. Uncensored hands, tied to the mafia or the Nordic gods offer manicured support. Eyes beckon and arms enclose malleable prey.

The rhythm beats on and I dance, barely stumbling. I am hard pressed to sleep for the sound is overwhelming. I am drugged and spinning round until the syncopation rescues my whirl and my head swings to the opposite and catches that beat. I am delightfully dizzy.

I gauge the depth of immersion on my ability to tread water and yet I ignore the warnings to stay close to shore. I swim in the sea of excess. The warm salty liquid holds me afloat and I bob on the waves. Sharks sniff at the honey drop caught in my oyster - the issue of risk's grit. Steel hulls of cruise ships carrying distracted bourgeoisie, pass me by, "starboard clear!" The pervasive threat to my pulsing perversions, the moral majority, is on board.

I am suffering from motion sickness. I yawn to recover my balance and clear my ears.

My Editor

We have come to Vancouver for the weekend. The night is starry on the deck overlooking the small private lake of our wealthy hostess. The tiny plastic jewelry bag of crystal dust, as it passes from one hand to the other, will be easily readable on her surveillance video cameras, sprinkled around her very valuable home. Our Patroness is 'using' as well. Most likely, so are the guards manning the mini televisions. Our eyes will glitter, foils indistinguishable from subjects.

My skirt is red, leather and tight. My red bra shows beneath my black Chinese silk blouse. My lips are red and wet and numb from too much attention.

My Editor is working on the story. He is in black leather with one brow raised surveying the possibilities. His cultivated disposition is injected with an underworld menace. He is like a scientist embarking on his experiment - the aim being to rearrange the molecular structure of the social group gathering around the pool table. He slips me the flap of blow and enters the oak room with the antique pool table taking center stage.

Soon, I join him at the pool table, prepared. We are not expecting gratification. We are seeking pleasure. Our aesthetic dominance is a distinguished disinterest. We are playing a silly ethnographic game.

The tipsy bisexual partner of La Patroness, our lesbian hostess, will be our target. She is called Brita.

Brita has high German cheekbones and white blonde hair. She has the masculine nuance that made Garbo appear so feminine, a brusque bravado with an inclination to throaty laughter.

My Editor suavely polishes Brita's potential. He briefs her on the playing positions and aims of the game. He insinuates the stakes.

"We are both after you, Justine and I, but you must win us." He tells Brita.

Her eagerness to win *him* is gauche. I temper her distorted ambition. I do this by assuming the role of her partner.

We play pool.

La Patroness and My Editor smoke the same cigar.

We, the dames, provide a visual counterpoint. We conspire, as girls do, and swear allegiance to each other. I encourage her excess and flirt mercilessly into her confidence. I sanction this duel with unethical curiosity.

Brita becomes silly putty. Her German demeanor wobbles at the knees.

La Patroness is beginning to sweat in the boy's room. She, like us, is enhanced in her perception - high and energized by Colombian mist. Only Brita is straight and drinking. Her eyelids are lowering under the strain of the alcohol.

I provide light banter as My Editor edits.

He plays pool. He sinks balls.

La Patroness, as well, plays with increasingly deadly ambition. She, too, sinks balls.

Brita is like a chicken, wings flapping in excitement. She is becoming famously flustered. Her feathers are ruffled. I have her half plucked. My Editor is buttering her up and will not let up. He is seducing Brita. When La Patroness protests and tries to censor the story, he disdains her attempts at agreeable morality. He justifies his ruthless tact with her histrionics for her past infidelities have loomed large around the bright green bed, rimmed by holes and supporting colorful balls. My Editor knows more about La Patroness than is good for her.

La Patroness twists the chalk on the cue end. Contortion breaks her handsome features. She shudders and lines up her cue as My Editor's forefinger presses the soft black fabric of Brita's pants from top to bottom, into the crack of her ample ass.

La Patroness shoots and sinks sad balls.

I begin to question the results of this game. I leave the table to buoy my bravado. I have possession of our packet of cocaine.

Back at the pool table, the insinuation of our intent bounces red shadows up from the cultivated green playing field onto our concentrated faces. La Patroness is tripping over the body of her piteous lesbian lover, Brita. My Editor is dealing cards so fast that the flurry of hands carries the sounds of an infestation.

Brita is seduced. Brita has fallen. We have only to decide to pick her up and take her home.

My Editor and I scan the statistical results of our social research. We decide Brita is not worth lifting up. She was damaged as she fell.

Tired of this game, we retire to our suite in the Tuscan style mansion. We are partners in crime and eye to eye we anoint each other's mettle. His flesh is chewable and I am able to dislodge great chunks, pulsing with vibrant red blood, from their hold on his frame. He attempts and teases response from categories meant for meandering. He raises his palm above the surface of my skin and draws forth an orgasm from my thigh. He parts the epidermal cells with his finger and enters my vital organs. I loose direction trying to keep up with his slow sensuous pace. He creeps up behind me and I explode on his tongue. I temper his steely heat to a patina of adoration. He brinks but never overflows. He groans and whispers. He tunes out, torques up and with my slippery vaginal skin sheathing his darting shaft, he advances forward, tickles, torments and tongue ties my warbling walls with pleasure. His chest is smothering me, his arms are protecting me from all evil, and his belly is warm. His ass is resonant on my palms as the vitality ascends from his balls towards yearning flesh tulips, towards a profusion of petals torn apart by desire. I clutch and squirt while he generates an energetic generous pulse. I accept everything, totally and loose myself to his benediction.

I am his thrall. I enclose my lips around his lucid manhood. I caress his softness. I entreat him to destroy me once again. I revive to entice obliteration.

He sleeps, in calm obedient comfort. I try to sleep, but my mind is racing. When I open my eyes, there is the tattoo on his shoulder describing his peculiar fetish, his distinction.

I am wired and rise to wander through the silent halls of the stately home. I am surprised to find La Patroness, in her study, as awake as I am. She beckons me over to her white marble desk. She has laid out a treasure of sensations. La Patroness is as loose as powder and, suffering from the aftermath of our deplorable behavior with Brita, she tells me her story - a continuum to the bits and pieces of abuse I have heard of, over the years of our friendship.

"There were twelve children in my father's family and nine in my stepmother's. Twenty-one children lived together in the same house. My father's children weren't allowed to stay inside in the daytime, summer or winter. We had to play or work outside of the big old farmhouse, (this was in Ireland, Justine, dirt poor, rocky, backwards, opinionated Ireland) which was eerily far from any other house. No neighbors and no outside friends made it conducive for Father to screw all of the girls, my stepsisters as well. Our brothers, once they were old enough, took over from Father.

When I was sixteen, I fell in love with a boy. I adored him, Justine. I absolutely and utterly loved him and I became pregnant. Father threatened this boy, demanding a shotgun solution.

My young man was frightened. He said that it wasn't his baby, that I had not been a virgin when he first had sex with me. Of course not - Father had screwed me first and then some of my brothers.

I had a different fear. I was afraid that if my baby was a girl, Father might fuck my daughter. So, I aborted the baby. My fears *were* justified for Father took my underage sister's baby from her, raised the child and screwed her, too. The child died."

"She died? How did she die?"

"I can't really say…

Eventually, as an adult, and because I was, by this time, a very rich woman, we took Father to court on an incest charge. I contacted my sisters and we demanded an acknowledgement and more, - an apology from Father. If he admitted to having had sex with us, we wouldn't pursue charges against him. We would only banish him from our lives and forget that we had been the issues of his evil loins.

By the time the preliminary hearing was in court, Father was a sick old man. He had cancer and was going to die. He walked with a cane - hunched and diminished. In the Prosecutor's office he denied all charges against him. He struggled up from his chair and drooled on his cane as he tried to slash at my face. He bombarded me with his familial lacerations. His anger was so intense that, had he not been held back by the police, he probably would have struck me with his rickety cane. One more blow could have fallen on top of the long history of blows he had already laid on me."

La Patroness breaks to bend over the mirror with the twenty dollar bill rolled and ready. She passes over to me.

"He was convicted but he died before he went to jail."

La Patroness became a nurse. She pioneered a program of home care for patients confined to wheelchairs. She hefted men twice her weight in and out of baths, wiped faces and was loved by her wards. It was with 'the quads' that she first used cocaine.

"The quads scored and I chopped - their hands shake spasmodically. Each morning, before I woke them, I would sequester myself, chop and snort. I discovered the means to limitless energy and physical strength. I would lift, chatter and scour for three more years before I met my husband and married him. He was fifty years my senior. He loved me unconditionally, as a father would – no sex. I was a confirmed lesbian by this time, never was with a man after that first young man, but this didn't bother him. He wasn't after me for sex. He died two years later. I fell back into this," and La Patroness gestures towards her desk top of white dust and paraphernalia, " to get through the loss."

La Patroness talks through a gram. It takes that long and she can't stop until it's all gone. She knows that she is right to do this and I know that I must be here and listen while she displays her tenacity. My being here is the excuse for her to continue drawing the dainty lines upon the precious mirror. Her chops and licks are justified.

She is my lesbian Butch bodyguard and with her forgiveness and protection; I launch my perfume.

The Dane

When My Editor and I arrive back in the valley, I say goodnight to him. I am tired of his chiding me for tooting and driving.

I rebel against all conscious discretion. I drive too fast up the hill, beyond the lights of the city. I pick up a bottle of wine and place it between my legs, so that as I press the gas and clutch pedals, I stave off the lust that craves attention. I detour with a digital exploration of my pink petals as I accelerate towards the clean country air.

The Dane has moved into one of the homes that overlook his log cabin below on the golf course. It is too cold for his trailer, too crisp for bon fires and cold outdoor showers. He is seated in an antique armchair that emphasizes his regal bearing. His Danish turquoise eyes are free of the impediments of care. His skin is bronze, taut across his cheekbones. His cock is erect with his pants at his ankles.

I hike up my skirt, pull my thong to one side and lower myself onto him.

Chapter Seven
Extrapolating Evil

My Editor

I will not see him for one immense week as he visits with his parents. I have not been invited.

I am breathing with difficulty, gulping back doubts of detoxification. I am in exile within my red room of hot memories, questioning the choice of hand in which to hold my teacup. I am confused as to where to set the temperature in my house. I cannot access domestic responsibilities. I fear financial ruin.

And so I cling to images of benediction.

I remember the night. We had retired from a mad whirl of oblique personalities powdered by cocaine. He was in my bed as I sought the comfort of my red, red room, having turned off the lights, destroyed the evidence - remnants of tiny folded envelopes, straws, dusty CDs, mirrors - and dampened the hearth fires. He flipped through the pages of *Art in America* with contempt.

The magazine slapped the Maplewood floor as he rolled onto his back and appraised my black stockings from beneath his hooded lids. His irises glistened with chemical inspiration. I straddled him. He took control. He maneuvered the lace and leather, the snaps and ribbons with contemplative unpeeling. He opened my blouse to reveal lime lace and pull out a nipple. He sucked the rosy berry. He searched out the inverted counterpart and brought the hesitant bud to full realization. Blouse fell to back. Bra unclipped by practice, dropped to his chest. As he slipped red leather over hips, my panties hitched a ride to the floor. The lacey-topped stockings remained. He had only to touch my vaginal petals and I swooned into the oblivion of my first coming. This was what he wanted.

Through smoky haze I watched as my hand squeezed his penis and my mouth accepted again and again his swollen manhood. I gagged at his thrusts. The muscles at the back of my throat clutched onto his engorged member until his cock rubbed the roof of my oral cavity raw. The skin seared from the heat of his virility. I was immersed in this activity, knowing only the language of internal combustion. When I glanced upwards, I idolized my discomfort.

As a falcon returns to the safety of a hooded enclosure, I returned again to come, in his mouth, on his palm - leaving sticky signatures on the sheets. The jousting continued through entrances and exits. The night was an intoxicating confusion of cataclysmic whispers. They told of promise and denial, of allegiance to royalty and the betrayal of family ties. They called me softly away from the cares that infest and delivered lisping messages of supple thighs and downy balls. The liquid release shuddered from his loins and spilled onto the small of my back to cool in the midnight, candlelit air.

I was in love with this sensation.

Tiny rivulets coursed over my sides as a mask of cum dried on my white back. The cloudy overflow, steamy hot from the innermost place of his sex, shimmered film on my spine.

I remembered this in totality before it was even past. A momentous moment was suspended.

But now I am banished and I languish in my exile. I am producing empty images over written erotica. I am too far away from his body to receive the clues necessary to continue. I voluntarily reduce the light of the present to a glowing cataract and cast about for glimpses of him passing by me. I am as alienated as Abraham was when God returned his sacrificial offering.

I am wasted and can't find my way home.

I am wading backwards in a shallow murky lake. As objects brush against my calf or squelch under my descending foot, I extrapolate significance from sensation.

I think back on the time when I first met Sebastian, My Editor's roommate, at that first gallery opening. I deducted from the undefined nuance between them that My Editor might be sleeping with Sebastian. I asked him. He answered in the negative and explained that Sebastian was a recovering alcoholic and drug addict. My Editor was careful to maintain sobriety in Sebastian's presence, respectful of his efforts. The shared custody of Sebastian's beautiful Eurasian son relies on this program of abstinence.

This explained the unique ambience between My Editor and the Russian student, Sebastian.

As time went on, we never brought alcohol or drugs to the clean dockside cottage where Sebastian and My Editor lived. We never mentioned our usage or left a trace of our weakness in the sequestered environment. I was invited to their house to sleep and have sex, only after Sebastian had left for Christmas.

One evening, at the close of the political campaign, as the election results were being discussed, My Editor requested a closed meeting with his party associates before we all rollicked into an evening of clubbing. Sebastian was out with us and we waited at the downstairs bar while the meeting was conducted above us. Sebastian ordered a beer, declaring it was his first drink in eight months. Overwhelmed by my associations with my ex-husbands binge drinking habits, I announced that I was not pleased to have been chosen as his compatriot on this auspicious occasion. I asked Sebastian if My Editor was aware of this nascent drop from sobriety.

Sebastian retorted. "There is no difference between me and Your Editor. He is just like me. I have known him for seventeen years. We are the same in this respect."

I am a relatively new dance partner and whether My Editor and I are two-stepping through 'nose candy' or waiting in uncomfortable silence for a connection to be made, I have been willing to tango. My Editor can call me at midnight and I dress to kill and come out to party. I can keep up, almost, - not drink for drink, but line for line, for I can retort a quick comeback, despite my many years of ascetic living.

When My Editor invites me to fly, I soar. The air currents buoy my body above all earthly concerns. I am liberal in my investment. I never reject his proposal. His impetus creates new reasons to spend. He beckons and I follow with an acute trust that when I duck under his umbrella I will not get wet. Rust will not dull my patina. My Editor's lesson is one of meticulous weeding out. He ascertains value and I trippingly trail on his judgment calls.

Now, as I retrace my steps, trying to place each retreating footfall in my previous marks, my over-sensitive soles sink into the warm mud. I look towards the lakeshore and indulge in interpreting vistas. I am detoxifying.

I review our habits.

After each miasma of social embraces, after the weekends in nightclubs, following the dinner parties with exceptional guests and as we bypassed a café on the last morning as I drove him home again - he would vow absolute abstinence and retreat. He would develop resentments for someone just met. Vague liaisons became betrayals. He had no faith in the process of small town great Gatsby's.

He backed off.

He incubated.

He pulled the dark hood forward and donned black shades. No one pierced his shroud. He was impervious.

I, admittedly, coaxed him back each weekend to lap a little more of life. We began our weekend on Thursday.

I arranged collectives. I paraded beautiful German women in front of him to seduce him away from his Eastern European discipline. I didn't follow his example of "eight hours sleep after a balanced diet of carbohydrates and proteins." No, I danced on my sugar rush. I became an after-hours athlete, refining the shape of my biceps and quads at the disco. I sent out for sparklers. I booked into group vacations with bad company. I issued gold leaf calling cards and held court in posh, decadent palaces.

My Editor and I no longer discussed the works of Derrida, Lacan and Neitsche. Instead, we negotiated contracts of accessibility to numerous partners, with discretion, and searched for the next source of cocaine.

This past week, as he's been driving in the car with his parents, the handbrake on our excess has been left on. It's been grinding the gears as the road from the past is traversed. His background is more present than I am. It shows now, how he's been to all the finest schools, sat through *Tosca, Aida, Carmen* and *Rigoletto* with his mother and discussed litigation with his father, first as a delicate boy, then as a pubescent punk and now as a man expected to produce grandchildren. And during *this* visit he has secretly detoxified under the distracted surveillance of his parents while I have detoxified under my own distracted surveillance.

I extrapolate that the evil My Editor must edit has nothing to do with a separation from the herd mentality. His chameleon covering is intact. He has the ability to identify with both the high and the low end of cultural research. The cross-hierarchical reference, which he steps into with alacrity, doesn't alter his ability to spell in his native language. He can operate in straight society while plugged into the underworld. His habits don't declare themselves.

He has spoken of his ability to compartmentalize. Does this mean he can wrap me up, Justine, his pretty plaything, in party paper with a label "some kind of trouble" and shelve me until I reappear on the pages of his next novel?

Or are my calves, as I wade backwards through the murk of detoxification, feeling hints that cleverly disguise their true nature?

Am I reading "flat-normal-ground" as "convoluted-pathway"?

The truth is subjective interpretation. There is the wafting scent of absolute potential but the omnipotent perspective is missing. Extrapolation, the line of an existing arc that logically can be extended, is at least comprehensible.

It's nothing to rely on, but its worthy of exploration. I extrapolate. I try and imagine who My Editor was before he walked into my life.

My Editor could also have been a recovering addict and alcoholic when I met him. I knew nothing of his past. I had surmised as we journeyed that he was the devil, the tempter, and I was to act as his racy consort. But the roles could have been reversed. My heels, high like tip-toe cloven hooves, tilt my pelvis forward and sway my back gracefully with the stance. I may have led with an ignorance of the steps but an intuitive sense of rhythm and movement. I didn't initiate purchase but I demanded stimulus. My eagerness to research, created an onus on My Editor, encouraging his excess.

For now it is *his* lipstick that is smeared and *his* eyelids that the diamonds have slipped from as he responds to his parental curfew.

And I too am suffering without him here, to scintillate me.

Dante

I must call Dante. I will inquire about the weather and ask him if his New York apartment is warm. I will allow my response to his resonance to build with my tutelage. I will dampen my sheets before nine on this steely gray wintry morning

My flushed face and beating heart are warning me of my appointment with surrender.

Chapter Eight
Trembling Trio

Juliette

My sister, Juliette, and I have talked about sharing lovers. We have discussed having an affair. In Venice, we conversed on the brink of my bed on a grappa wave, relating our past experience or lack of it. She had sex with her girlfriend at twenty-one and lost the friendship to an uncomfortable silence. I have never been with a woman but I fantasized and projected the lingering sensations I would perform upon her body. We talked of the pleasure I would receive from her and she from me.

I have not wanted a lesbian lover, but a woman with whom I could share a man and through his common bondage gain access to a female lover. Juliette, my sister, is my first choice and often an alternate subject of desire for my male lovers as well. My ex-husband, Tiziano, The Dane and now My Editor - we all have wanted Juliette.

Tiziano savored my suggestion that we invite Juliette into our illegitimate liaison. Juliette rolled the taste of Tiziano on her tongue and it was this provocation that had brought her to my bedside in Venice. We spoke of the potential but retained a delicious, shy, sisterly distance.

My Canadian letter writer, Ben, the man whose huge member held me in thrall for many months, also fancied Juliette. At this time she was reinforcing her monogamous leanings under the spell of a beautiful young lover, a musketeer. *He* had asked *her* for *me*. He wanted to try on his lover's sister and languish in the dreams of *my* scent, but Juliette was too much in love to share him.

The Dane met Juliette and again I suggested that we arrange a threesome. His lyrical articulation, stunning body and white blonde peach fuzz enticed Juliette. She was struck by the lightening bolt of his exceedingly good looks. But she waffled, having turned to a previous ex-lover who eclipsed her musketeer, and it was too complicated.

My Editor eclipses The Dane. Now we are plotting our way into Juliette's bed.

Juliette, for she is my sister, knows all of my secrets, except those of my physical body. She knows who my lovers are and have been and what we do sexually to each other; I, reciprocally, know the same of her sexual exploits. Five minutes after she accepted the doctor back into her bed, while her beautiful musketeer charged off on his prancing steed, she touched herself as she related to me her guilt and we came together over the telephone. I knew how her ex-lover, the doctor, entered her and the dirty deviations she accepted. She had told me, as well, tales of the musketeer and his many portals of entry.

Juliette has heard from me, how My Editor flutters his cock between my successive orgasms deep in the folds of pulsation and brings me to yet another excruciating ecstasy.

Juliette and I may leave each other verbally panting; but we have yet to touch each other's breasts, smell our reciprocal liquids or kiss.

My Editor follows the nuance.

We meet Juliette backstage. She's wearing a red satin dress crusted with gold and her breasts are pushed to a cleft of glowing white skin. We are a trembling trio. Juliette is a spurt of strawberry on an iced confection. My Editor is scraped, as if he carried the scars of a recent battle. Juliette and I like this look.

We take Juliette to the bathroom with a drugged suggestion to consider.

Yes, we talk and we talk - Juliette and I. She has decided to accept my offer to share. It must be kept a secret from the doctor and the musketeer, who, in praising the taste and texture of her sex, created a longing, in Juliette, for mine. She has become curious as to what I feel like. She knows what she likes and she wants to know if I like the same. Now, she wants to feel me.

A code of absolute loyalty must be maintained. We are after all, closer to each other than to our lovers. We are sisters. Juliette and I will arrange the meeting.

We talk about it on the couch in my living room over a glass of wine. We rest our legs across each other, hers in wine leather, and mine in black silk with sparkles. We decide that when she returns from Florida and I from New York, we will do it.

Chapter Nine
Edited Out

The Dane

I look back through the pages and I discover a disappearance. I find that which is no longer there. I trip on he-who-is-missing. He has been around and about. He has been implied, but The Dane has been censored.

My Editor is always present and I believe that this body of ethnographic research into *the limits of love and knowledge* is no longer an independent intimate project, for the medium is mixing with the message as it is made. Editing is superimposed on creating and that which should come last with clarity of distance is, instead, cutting images around and into the celluloid as it captures the moment. As I, Justine, the scriptwriter and My Editor become one entity of inquiry, the supporting actors are canned, right, left and center. Cyclopean vision interprets action.

The Dane's disappearance doesn't alter the narrative. It is in tact. There is a logical sequence of events. The Dane's presence is just no longer necessary to the story line. The Dane walks a last walk down the catwalk alone, as My Editor hands me up onto the stage in a new red outfit. Then he leaves. He drives away and waves from across the street as My Editor smokes out front.

I have made appointments with the Dane. I had all intentions of keeping them, but I cancelled. Now, I lie awake at night wondering about him as I sleep with My Editor, hanging onto his back.

I am consumed with interest in this new field of research, My Editor. This library is immense. I wander from political theory and spirituality, to tantric sex and drugs, to self help and sociological constructs. I loose track of the floor plan and become lost in the stacks.

I don't see, I don't smell and I don't even hear a rumor that the books are burning. The legends of Thyra, the stories of the Vikings and the tales of pirates are all scattered as ashes and become indistinguishable. Is this flaking fall-out or fertile soil? The Dane is about to embark on that expected journey homeward to his baby in her wooden cradle, rocked by the Northern Sea. His ship is in the harbor and supplies are being loaded on board. I don't have an evening left open to jump on his hook. I doubt that I will again bounce, surreptitiously, on his strong-man thighs. For now, I will forego the seduction of his baby blue eyes and blonde peach fuzz. I have learned to survive without him in my life even while he has been knocking at my door.

My head has been so deep in this book that I am writing that I failed to notice that the Dane had been edited out.

Chapter Ten
Questions at the Border

I am a generation older than my lover, My Editor. His parents are a generation older than me, forty years older that their son. My lover, The Editor, is twice as old as *my* youngest son. My son has written an essay titled "Bullying" that included this phrase: "people suffer prejudice against their race, sex, class and age."

I have been told by my lover that we endure scathing stares, incredulity and righteous raising of brows. He claims to have been challenged by judgmental contumely because of our age difference.

I, the progressive optimist, look at his physical being with calm and equality. From behind these wrinkled lids, I, too, am young, inspired, idealistic and "in great shape." My energy is undaunted. I have no trouble keeping up. I read the stares, for heads *do* turn, mouths gape open and silence descends upon our entrances. It is admiration at our aspects. It happens when I walk alone. I stand out from a crowd, not by virtue of my beauty, for I can analyze my features objectively, with humility. I believe the attention is a result of the inescapable nakedness that I display. I wear my blithe heart on my sleeve and the public do not believe my claim to being clothed. I give this impression willingly. I have developed it as a bridge over the generation gap.

My Editor is walking nude as well. Despite his immaculate presentation, his evident good taste and badges of breeding, he doesn't ring true. He carries a familiar intimacy that pleads for recognition. Onlookers stretch their minds to review television personalities, politicians and notorious criminals, trying to place his elusive aura in a comfortable context. They fail. The fog of intrigue lingers on his frame and enhances his attraction. Budding young women root to the ground in confused disbelief, stupidly wandering through the possibilities of closure on the stunning apparition.

There is a prejudicial response to our presence as individuals. In combination the impression is more potent. We endure it rather than react to it. We live inside our superior mystery. We have created it by risking our lives to be who we are. The public attention is a mild by product of danger. Each of us is deviant and it shows. We are artists.

On the dance floor, an awkward drunk wedges My Editor back towards the gaping crowd. My editor's arm jerks and fist punches stomach flab. The hip night-set clears an exit path for us. Their gaze sweeps from my petite posturing to My Editor's towering threat. The band resumes as the bouncers drag a floored, pudgy body, the awkward drunk, from the circle of twinkling ovals cast by the mirror ball. No one challenges My Editor's authority - not the Angels at the back bar, the owner or the decent offended patrons.

We have gone back to our toxic habits and haunts.

Next night at the club a woman asks My Editor to dance as I stand with him at the bar. She offers her name and shows him her badge. She alludes to having sex up her ass with her boots left on and the light blue cotton shirt open to display her amazing breasts. She invites him for a morning coffee and then sex in the cruise car parked in front of the police station with his transfigured face the only hint for the sergeant looking out the station window at the blow job being performed in the parked patrol car.

My Editor gives her his business card and tells me of her solicitations.

We are followed too close for proximity comfort as we leave the club. My Editor pushes aside my safely clasped hand. Back bristling and hard heels strike a purposeful direction past the biker bar. Renegade pellets have blown out the street lamps and in the sooty black patch, we are surrounded. Pocketed guns brush my panic and then drop off through the swinging side doors of boisterous inclusion.

He'd freed his hands to reciprocate the intimidation and we pass unharmed.

We continue and arrive at our destination, the Bistro, with a project to score.

When our connection arrives at the Bistro with a delivery, there is an ultimatum.

"Ask!"

I feel that I am being pressured into asking the question. My Editor had been receiving powdered beneficence, our cocaine crutch, because *I* had recommended him. Yet *I* knew nothing of My Editor until he had come forward, having traced his

147

eyes down the crack of my bum, past the thong on my Harley pictured on a city calendar, eight months ago. I had thought then that he was shady.

I am now absolutely complicit in his shadiness. I realize that he engages in espionage. He records conversations. He plays a shark's game of pool and slowly leaks out his credentials. We all recognized him, but no one could place the original context.

They had sent babes to tempt him away from me. They tried a variety of models. The teenage daughter of the guitarist planted her firm nubile legs astride his lap and begged to be fondled. The lesbian lover chased his exits with her email address, home phone, cell phone and invitations to go boating, - all forming a flag of desire fluttering in his wake. The busty blues singer rubbed her tits on his chest as she sought a light for her smoke. She offered to be used from any direction and in any orifice just to have his baby. The Italian designer rested her thigh against his and curled her toe into his crotch.

The latest temptation was the cop at the club.

He didn't have to tell me any of this. I witnessed it all.

He says he has never betrayed me.

But now Carlotta, the dealer, is making demands. She asserts she has identified My Editor. She wants an introduction and an assurance before she hands over our "treat." And thus, I am called upon to ask, for I know more about him than any one else.

Yet I know no more than I can touch with my palms spread above his surfaces in a room as dark as indifference. I know the speed of his thrusts. I have numbed my tongue to his and joined his throat dripping a seductive highlight. I know his sexual appetite and the feel of his young cock against my ass as the morning light shows too much of my age.

Yes, it's logical that *I* should ask him.

But despite my inside track and the glimpse of his barbarian intellect, I had not anticipated his answer.

I have to deal with it. The question is general now, not specific.

The topic is betrayal and with whom do our loyalties lie?

I am on the plane now, back to New York. I have left him to play out his story without me.

I was his partner in an extreme espionage. When I was most effective, I had no idea of the role I was playing or the power I was wielding.

Will I still be punished if I know nothing? Will they track me down?

Epilogue

My sister, Justine, has always been a worry to me. I thought that if I documented her libertine lifestyle, with all her amorous adventures, I might get a handle on the enigma.

But I haven't figured her out. I can only, barely, discern her philosophy.

Justine *means* to stand for freedom. She has the idea that through researching the limits of love and knowledge, she will discover some kind of truth and hand it back to humanity.

She has taken tremendous risks. Her Editor, for instance, a man whom she suspected from the beginning - was he good for her? Could he have been dangerous?

For, Justine suffered a set back. A little too dependant on cocaine, she returned to New York City. I'm not sure if she experienced a healing, a purging or a resurrection there.

She told me that it could be summed up with this statement: "Juliette," she said with that ever-believing, wide-eyed smile, "I used to have a lump in my throat about who it was that I *was*, what it was that I *did*, my *authenticity*. I no longer have that lump, Juliette. I no longer feel *bad* or *scared*."

I wrote an article after Justine had been found by a desk clerk in a sleazy hotel with her throat slashed from ear to ear. Justine survived, partially due to the clerk's ingenuity. He taped her neck wound shut with packing tape and called an ambulance. I have included an excerpt from the article, documenting the investigations. I was grateful that it wasn't a bigger story than what it turned out to be. She was, after all, an heiress. I could have been the reporter making a million from the exclusive story of a famous murder.

But I, thank God, wasn't! And I am not a reporter. I am a writer with a great concern and respect for a dear sister, nothing more.

Here, then, is the excerpt:

The desk clerk at the National Hotel raised his gaze above the swipe of Justine Quercia's gold card to ask if she would be spending the night. His discreet lids and sufficiently servile neck discounted identification.

The hookers in the elevator switched their weight from stiletto spike to spike, chewing sugary gum and noticing nothing above the belt buckle of a stranger, a young, enigmatic man with e red head leaning against his side.. They remember seeing her. But all they remember of him was the impression of his stud swagger, as the couple exited the elevator.

149

They were in room 42.

During the trial Justine said that she had watched him pee in the bathroom. She had been moved to go over and wrap her arms around his waist and flick the soft skin at the end of his penis to dislodge the golden drops. He was still dressed. She hadn't felt a weapon.

Yes, she had known where she was. Through the cardboard walls the moans of the prostitutes enforced the morality of the moment of take-and-be-taken. With her hands pinioned to her spine by his sax player's span, the difference between decency and mounting a minion had dissolved. The crisis persisted in a question of living or dying.

The prostitutes had heard Justine crying out behind the thin walls. Some of them thought it was in agony, some thought it was drugged, although most of the women who were questioned acted dumb. They didn't want to acknowledge that they might know the difference.

One said that Justine "was leaving her body with feeble consent, to surrender to an orgasm."

The possibility of murder shone as an answer to time passing and a myriad of decisions to make, for most of these ladies of the night.

"She shrieked like a perforated banshee and then it sounded as if she shuddered, as if she was climbing her way back to air fit to breathe," testified another painted lady.

The division between potential and annihilation had apparently already disappeared. His disinterested masterful strokes had ruled out the distinction that made" living" the only priority.

When they came to interrogate the desk clerk, as to whether it had, indeed, been Justine who had checked in with the handsome young man on November 11, the clerk based his positive recognition on all that he had registered in that frame between the visa machine and the soft hollow at the base of her neck.

Justine said that the hollow had concealed a lump in her throat.

Justine survived the gash from ear to ear. Perhaps the lump rolled under the bed in the sleazy night, for despite her evident abuse, she would not testify against the young man.

She said, "I have no idea who he might have been. He was a complete stranger to me, a sax player. He said that he had sucked off men for money.

Yes, I signed for the room. He didn't have a visa card."

The above is an excerpt from the article "Sax Player becomes Sex Slayer," as it appeared in *TREND Magazine*, written by Juliette Quercia, the sister to Justine Quercia.

Stolen Statements

The italicized passages on the noted pages are from the following sources:

Page 7 - Justine Quercia, "Personal Mandate"
Page 8 - Jacques Lacan
Page 10 - Andy Grafitti, "The Pillow Book" and John Donne's "The Rake's Progress"
Page 37 - William Butler Yeats, "Leda and the Swan"
Page 53 -Jacques Derrida
Page 41 - a paraphrase of the introduction to Dante's *Inferno*
Page 73 - Henry Wadsworth Longfellow, "The Day is Done"
Page 78 - paraphrase of Henry Wadsworth Longfellow, "The Day is Done"
Page 77- Martin Heidegger
Page 85 - A Pop Song from the 70's
Page 90 - Jacques Derrida
Page 122 - Dostoevsky *Notes from Underground* and Justine Quercia, "Personal Mandate"
Page 126 - an instructional manual, "How to Draw Animals"